Job
The Cornerstone
of the Universe

a novel by
John Passfield

Rock's Mills Press
Oakville, Ontario
2017

Published by
ROCK'S MILLS PRESS
All rights reserved. Published by arrangement with the author.

Cover illustration: The cover illustration is a painting by William Blake: *The Ancient of Days (God Creating the Universe)*, 1794.

Cover design: Craig Passfield

Author's website: www.johnpassfield.ca

ISBN-13: 978-1-77244-079-9

Chapter 1

Alone on the ash-heap.
A man who enjoys great favour in the eyes of God.
I am the leper in whom is the plague. My clothes are rent. My head is bare. I am defiled. I dwell alone on the edge of the village. I scatter ashes over my head. I tear my garments into shreds. I beat my chest and wail. I send my torment straight to the ears of God.

My skin is on fire. My life is in ashes. My children are dead.

Naked came I from my mother's womb.

The earth was without form and void.
Darkness was upon the face of the deep.
The spirit of the Lord hovered over the waters.

Naked shall I return.

Tending to the needs of my flocks and my herds.
Overseeing the preparations of my travelling caravans.
Enjoying my three daughters and my seven sons.

The Lord giveth and the Lord taketh away. Blessed is the name of the Lord.

Is every one of your children dead?
Seven sons and three daughters?
How could this be?

Alone on the ash-heap.
A man who is the greatest of all the men of the East.

1

A roof has collapsed. I have lost every one of my children. I have covered myself in ashes. I mourn my great loss. I brush aside the words of my friends. I demand to have an interview with God himself. Why, I want to ask, has this been allowed to happen? What kind of a world has God wrought? How are we to live in it? Why does God not come down – calipers in hand – and tell us what he wants us to think?

God is greater than man.

We hope.

Double to win. Double to win.
This is my motto. Double to win.
The choice is between the skull or the skin.
This is my motto. Double to win.

Only a few days ago. The morning sun is gradually warming up the air. I pause and drink at a well.

Checking my fields and livestock. The nearest and farthest fields. A long ride, beginning at sunrise. The expectation of a tiring day.

My eldest son sends word as I sip the cold water. My sons and my daughters are eating and drinking wine today in my eldest son's house. I am flattered by the invitation, and keep the messenger waiting while I consider what words I wish to send. How to explain how busy I am? How one doesn't manage the feed and care of seven thousand sheep, of three thousand camels, of five hundred yoke of oxen, of five hundred she-asses, of a very great household, of one of the foremost establishments of one of the greatest men of the east, by eating and drinking wine with one's children in the house of one's eldest son? I send the messenger off with my words. My blessing on all my children. If only I were as carefree as they seem to be. I will sanctify them with offerings, of course, but my attendance will have to depend on the needs of the day. Suddenly, there is a shout. My fellow travellers respond to the cry. A rider is clamouring in the distance. Shouting something that I have to strain to hear.

Eating and drinking wine - a cry from inside the house - thou hast shewed thy people hard things - naked came i - the misfortune of the pious - incline thine eare unto me - why standeth thou afar off, o lord - interview with god - oxen plowing and asses feeding - absolutely unprovoked by sin.

"The oxen were plowing, and the asses were feeding beside them! And the Sabeans fell upon them and took them away! They have slain thy servants with the edge of the sword! I only am escaped alone to tell thee!"

My God, my God, why hast thou forsaken mee? Why art thou so far from helping me, and from the words of my roaring?

O my God, I crie in the day time, but thou hearest not; and in the night season, and am not silent.

Alone on the ash-heap.

A man who one day feels the edge of the sword.

Am I dreaming? Can such things come to pass? Can all of these things be happening to me? I wonder if anyone can help me. Please tell me if there is a rising, a scab or a bright spot in the skin of my flesh? Does it look like it might be the plague of leprosy? Have I been brought unto the priest? Has he looked at my skin? Has the priest pronounced me to be unclean?

Behold God is great and we know him not.

Neither can the number of his years be searched out.

We fear.

A tree grew in the forest.

It reached its leaves towards the sky.

But it never got there.

Many years ago. When Eliphaz and I were both young men.

The two of us standing and talking at a well. On a trading trip to the land of our old friend, Baruch.

A young girl approaches. She carries a jug on one shoulder. She stops and stands a number of feet from us and doesn't move. I break off and turn from Eliphaz. I call out softly to the girl. If you wish to use the well, we shall move away. We are merely chattering idly. Our thirsts are quenched. She stands her ground, a number of feet from us. The jug remains on her shoulder. She doesn't move. I will wait. I am not in a hurry. You may take your time. She is wearing an earth-coloured robe and her feet are bare. We are here to meet with Baruch. He said to meet him at the well. We are traders and we come from other lands. Baruch is my father. I am sure he will be here soon. He would not want me to displace you. I only want water. My errand can wait. I take Eliphaz by the arm and move him away. We will stand there, under the shade. It is too hot here to stand and talk. Please feel free to get your water. If you leave the jug by the well, we will fill it for you. She approaches the well and leaves the jug. She moves away and stands and waits. I leave Eliphaz and go to the well and fetch up the pail. I pour the water into the jug and move away. She approaches and raises the jug to her shoulder. Thank you, kind sir. You are very generous. Perhaps my father has been detained. If I see him, I shall remind him that you and your friend await him at the well.

Forming myself out of clay.
Granting audience to those who would speak with me.
Giving an account of all my matters.

"This must be the eldest daughter of Baruch. A gentle young lady."
"There was no need for us to monopolize the well."
"The kind of daughter who would make a father proud."

All of your children gone in an instant?
A great wind came out of the wilderness?
How can such things be?

Alone on the ash-heap.
A man whose beasts and servants are lost and destroyed.
I am wracked by fever. I am tormented by boils. I am devastated by the loss of my entire family. I cry out to the heavens. Why has my God forsaken me? Why do such things happen here on earth? Why is the universe so flawed? Why are human beings subjected to such agonizing torments? I shake my fist at the sky. I demand a personal audience. My agony gives me questions. I insist on hearing the answers from the mouth of God.

The mountains are always there. They were there long before us. They will be there long after we pass away.

In the beginning God created the Heauen, and the Earth.

A little boy brings scraps of food. A few pieces of meat in a wooden bowl and a pitcher of water.
I eat from the bowl as he pours the water into my flask.
Who is this little boy? Not my grandson, that is for sure. All of my children's children perished when the house collapsed.

Alone on the ash-heap.
A man's sons and daughters drinking wine.
My wife and all of our children. The days that we have known. The nights when we have thought there would be no end. God made the flowers that bloom in the oasis. Why did he make the man who slakes his thirst at the well? The agonizing, aching desire to hold fast to that which is good. To our parents, to our spouses, to our children, to our friends. To the

drops of dew on the morning flowers. To the colour of the wheat-field in the breeze. Why is all this given to us? Why is all of this taken away? What does the blood that lives in my body seem to mean?

Thou shalt have thy delight in the Almighty.
Thou shalt lift up thy face unto God.

We rejoice.

You say that you want to talk, my brother.
Though silence was golden before.
It is words that leave the deepest wounds.
I would rather you use a knife.

As long ago as I can remember. Somewhere far in the past. Myself a babe in arms. A dark night. A glowing fire. The stars above.

My whole village is sitting around the campfire. It is my village, my family, my tribe. One person will chant some words and the whole village will chant in reply. The ashes are stirred. More wood is placed on the pile. The fire grows stronger. The logs burn brightly. The faces glow. The voices are soothing. The elders chant. They take their turns. They lead the worship. We chant in reply. A chorus of voices. We sing to the hills. The faces of my siblings. The faces of my parents. The faces of my grandparents. All glowing in the light of the fire. Chanting psalms in the night. Chanting psalms that reach to heaven. Chanting psalms to each other and to God.

Blackened and burning carcases - witnesses of the creation - preserve me, o god - the morning sun - women and children weeping - if mules were human - the most to be dreaded of sins - as carefree as they seem - I have set the lord always before me - when i am old and gray headed - sheep and servants consumed by fire.

"Make a joyful noise unto the Lord, all ye lands. Serve the Lord with gladness. Come before his presence with singing."

"Know ye that the Lord he is God. It is he that hath made us, and not we ourselves. We are his people, and the sheep of his pasture."

"Enter into his gates with thanksgiving, and into his courts with praise. Be thankful unto him, and bless his name. For the Lord is good. His mercy is everlasting, and his truth endureth to all generations."

Ancient calipers of brass and of wood.
God created the heavens and the earth.

5

The Lord God formed man of the dust of the earth.

Alone on the ash-heap.
A man's children lying dead in a broken house.
I am alive in every moment. Every moment is fiercely painful. Every moment is agony to me. If only I were unaware of the aching in my heart. If only I were unaware of the beating of my brain. Fierce fires rage in my bloodstream. Painful memories arise before my eyes. Paralyzing consciousness. I don't know how I can go forward. If only my essence could cease to be. Pain is my only fuel. Pain is the single fuel that propels me through my days.

All they that see me, laugh me to scorne: they shoote out the lippe, they shake the head, saying,
He trusted on the Lord, that he would deliuer him. Let him deliuer him, seeing he delighted in him.

We mourn.

Chatting cheerfully in the marketplace.
Offering advice in the gatherings of the elders.
Worshipping the one who is greater than I.

A few days ago. The morning sun is gaining strength.
The fields where my oxen were plowing. The surviving servant showing me over the site.
The oxen were ploughing, Master! And the asses were feeding beside them in the grasses here! And the Sabeans came upon us! They came stealthily, like thieves in the night! Your servants fought them bravely! They were slain with the edge of the sword! I only escaped to tell thee! Signs of scuffling and pools of blood. Knives and spears dropped in the furrows. The bodies of my servants wrapped in linen. Women and children weeping. A whistle from a distance. A messenger, Master, coming up the road! It is hard to tell who it is, but I recognize the burro as one of yours!

A young shepherd had a wise friend.
The wise friend gave the young shepherd advice.
If ever you are menaced by a fierce wolf, reach out and stroke him under the chin.
He will become placid. Almost a friend.

"The fire of God is fallen from heaven, and hath burned up thy sheep and thy servants and consumed them! I only am escaped alone to tell thee!"

A great wind from the wilderness - curse god and die - all scrupulosity of life - our thirsts are quenched - as for god, his way is perfect - a temporary chastisement - god made the flowers - save me from the lion's mouth - a man with a blessing to give - seven sons and three daughters.

Alone on the ash-heap.
A man's wife advising that he curse God and die.
Many have tried to comfort me. What does any of them know? The village elders? The priests? My wife? Their words are empty for me. There is nothing that they can say. I want no one to sit by my side on this ash-heap. I want no comfort from men. As ashes are the words of solicitous friends.

A man stands on a mountain top and looks out over a plain. His eyes are filled with wonder. A man of hopes, a man of vision, a man of dreams.

Seven sons and three daughters.
Feasting and telling stories in their brother's house.
A great wind arising from the wilderness.

Will I ever see my hopes fulfilled? Will I ever know my vision? Will I ever live to see my dreams come true?

I am powred out like water, and all my bones are out of ioynt. My heart is like waxe. It is melted in the middest of my bowels.
My strength is dried vp like a potsheard, and my tongue cleaueth to my iawes, and thou hast brought me into the dust of death.

A land of milk and honey. A land of abundance. A land he has been told is the promised land.

There is only one whose words I would care to hear. I yearn for a visit from my old friend, Barachel. The only person that I would wish to see.
A man of complete understanding. A man in tune with my every thought. I wish that he were sitting here beside me.
Surely he will come, in my agony, to comfort me.

Every son and every daughter?
What would cause such a thing to happen?
Is there a cause or is this disaster a random event?

We pray.

Alone on the ash-heap.
A man sitting on an ash-heap with a tattered dream.
My children! My children! My children! Mattan and the ruined grain! Jemima and the caravans! Heber and the widow! Epher and the sandstorm! Bazak and the golden land! Kezia and her choices! Evron and the bleating lamb! Avram and the coughing lion! Noach and the mystery! Keren and the bucket at the well! Oh my children! My children! My children! To have all of them given to me! To have all of them taken away! What is the plan that engenders such agony as this?

Chapter 2

Trudging along the street in heaven! It is a wide avenue that stretches ever upwards towards a palace! There are no streets intersecting on either side! There is a wide expanse of paving stones! Travellers have spoken of such wonders in fabled cities! There are many large public buildings! Vast and looming overhead! Perhaps a ministry of the good and a ministry of the wicked! Each with an angel who has been placed in charge! But then why so many buildings? And why so vast in scale? They dwarf the human figure into nothingness!

Man that is born of woman is of few days and full of trouble.

A long trek over difficult terrain.
A shepherd waving a flaming brand.
A man teasing his serious friend.

He cometh forth like a flower and is cut down. He fleeth as a shadow and continueth not.

Bringing mankind forth out of the womb.
Bringing hidden things to light.
Giving understanding to the heart.

His days are determined. The number of his months are not in his hands. Bounds have been appointed that he cannot pass.

Why such fears of falling asleep?
Do we not dream while we are awake?
Are not our greatest fears revealed by our open eyes?

Trudging along the street in heaven! A vast avenue which leads to a palace! What am I walking on? Is this gold beneath my feet? Paving stones made of gold? I stop walking and get down on my knees! It certainly seems to be gold! I press my thumbnail into the surface and press and press! Gold! Yes! It is gold, sure enough! But why would the streets of heaven be paved with such a surface as gold? Gold is soft and does not wear well! It could never bear the traffic! It would wear out under the footfalls of so many sandals and the paving stones would constantly need to be replaced!

God openeth men's ears to deception.
He commands that they return from iniquity.

We laugh.

A man and a dog in the forest.
Each chooses a different path.
Each looks at the other; neither blinks.
Am I the master here or are you?

A day or so ago. The afternoon at its height. The heat is quite oppressive.
The fields where I kept my sheep. The surviving servant showing me over the site.
It came as fire from the heavens, Master! We were moving the sheep into pens! The dogs were herding the flocks! The men were rounding up strays! I felt a blinding flash and I tumbled into a ditch and fell unconscious! When I awoke, I rubbed my eyes! There were carcases all around me! Blackened and burning as if in a fire! My fellow servants had perished as well, Master! All had suffered the fate of the sheep! I only managed to survive! I only was able to escape and come to tell you! Carcases of sheep and dogs all lying on the ground. Burnt flesh and fur and wool stinging my nostrils. My servants' bodies wrapped in linen. Their wives and children bewailing their loss. A shout from down the road. I will run to see who it is, Master! Perhaps someone from another field! We can only hope that nothing else is amiss!

His mighty acts - the weather looks fine - the secret of god is in my tent - an anxious dread of offending god - I will wash mine hands in innocency - so vast a scale - the root grows old in the earth - greatest fears revealed - hear the voice of my supplications - fundamental critical questions.

"The Chaldeans made out three bands and fell upon the camels and have carried them away! They have slain thy servants with the edge of the sword! I only am escaped alone to tell thee!"

The heauens declare the glory of God: and the firmament sheweth his handy worke.
Day vnto day vttereth speach, and night vnto night sheweth knowledge.

Trudging along the street in heaven! The hill is steep and I am out of breath! I force myself to climb! I will soon be seeing God! I try to think of all the things I would like to ask! Why are there murderers, thieves and pickpockets? Why do widows suffer indignities? Why do orphans pick-over ash-heaps? Why are old people hungry and cold? Climbing the hill of heaven! Moving towards the palace as fast as I can! I am desperate to ask my questions! Why is there rain when there is plenty? Why is there drought when there is need? Soon I will have my audience with God!

Thou shalt know that thy tabernacle shall be in peace.
And thou shalt visit thy habitation and shalt not sin.

We cry.

A man was alone on the desert.
He cursed his vile luck.
I am a scorpion, he said to himself.
There are no people here for me to sting.

Bildad and I as partners. Many years ago.
Sipping cold water and hatching our plans in the shade.
Bildad proposes a plan. He has heard of a land where there is famine. A two-week trek from here by caravan. There is drought in the land of Uz, and in the land of the Shuhites too, but there is a much more terrible famine in the land of Elath. Why don't we combine our resources and sell our grain in the land of the famine? I have heard that grain sells there at more than twice the price. We could put the grain in sacks, as we do when we go to market, and make a caravan of mules and hire some drivers, and even buy up some extra grain. Then, when we get to the land where there is famine, we could sell the grain and the mules.

Evaluating ewes in the pens.
Visiting friends in other lands.
Checking a camel's hoof.

"Think of the fortune that we could make! We would each of us have a nest-egg to build up our holdings!"

"Our lands are only two days apart! One of us could go and one of us could stay! One could oversee both our holdings and one could take the grain to the market and make the sale!"

"We could draw straws to see who would stay and who would go!"

What is the function of dreams?
Are there people who never dream?
Are dreams and nightmares different or are they the same?

Trudging along the street in heaven! Approaching the palace at the top of the hill! All of the buildings seem to have murals! Some are carved into the sandstone and some are painted on the marble! Seven golden lamp-stands! Seven stars held in a hand! A hand holding a key! Feet glowing as in a furnace! A carving of rushing waters! I catch my breath as I scan the murals! A tree standing alone! A man with a robe and a golden sash! Twenty-four figures on twenty-four thrones! A lion, a fox, a man and a flying eagle! A scroll with seven seals! I cannot tell what any of it means! I turn and continue my journey on the heavenly avenue!

The desert sands are always shifting. They are like the waves of the sea. Waves of sand engulf and waves of sand recede.

And the earth was without forme, and voyd, and darkenesse was vpon the face of the deepe: and the Spirit of God mooued vpon the face of the waters.

I never used to dream. Or if I did, I would never remember what I had dreamed of when the morning came.

Trudging along the street in heaven! There are questions I want to ask! Why does the sun come up in the morning? Why does the sun go down at night? Why are animals born in the springtime? Why does rain make flowers grow? I am tired! My legs are weary! I pause for breath! Why do brigands rule the highways? Why does death come early to some? Why are widows cast aside like so much trash!

God will not hear vanity.
Neither will the Almighty regard it.

We wonder.

A cobbler makes sandals in the marketplace.
The finest leather, the finest needles, the finest thread.
Everyone admires the sandals that he makes.
Word spreads up and down the caravan trails.

Many years ago. When I was just a very tiny boy.
A cool night. All of us gathered together. The only sound is the crackling of the fire.

I am in my mother's arms. We are sitting around a fire. My father's father, my grandmother, my father and my mother and all my siblings. My father's father is a shepherd, and we are in the fields. We sleep in tents at night. My grandfather and my father will sleep at the gate of the sheep-fold, in order to protect the sheep from predators. Wolves are always on the alert and shepherds must be even more alert than the keenest wolf. We listen to my father's father as he talks. My grandmother sits at his side as he tells stories of the days when he used to be a young man. There is wisdom in his stories. Everyone in the family listens quietly. I was surrounded by a pack of wolves! Perhaps a dozen, maybe more! I had to protect my precious sheep! My father was counting on me to protect them! The wolves were growling and snarling! They were grinning and showing their fangs! They were circling all around me! I stood at the gate of the pen! I waved a flaming brand, like this, that I take from the fire!

No one should have to suffer - the questions of the community - thy hand was heavy upon me - I would like to ask - a very different point of view - done as you should have done - what profit is there in my blood - draw straws to see - rise up to the heavens - an unsatisfactory theology.

"We are shepherds, always shepherds. As far back as anyone knows. For all time, our family has tended sheep."

"The sheep have been good to us. Through the good times and the bad. We could do worse than be the people who tend the sheep."

"From the time that I was an infant. From the time that I was a boy. The only life I have known has been that of a shepherd."

A whole village filled with praise for a very young girl.
A lamb in danger of being eaten by wolves.
Two men having a talk beside a lagoon.

Trudging along the street in heaven! I can see no people here! An endless avenue! Vast public buildings! Gigantic murals! But there are no travellers on the streets! I see no one climbing ahead of me as I make my way to the palace! I see no one as I turn and look behind! The avenue goes on forever behind me and disappears in the mist! Is everyone at the palace? Is this God's visiting day? Will I find angels and messengers in the throne room reporting to God! And what about my ancestors? My grandparents and my parents? My departed brother and sister? Will I get to speak to them? Will they be there?

There is no speach nor language, where their voyce is not heard.
Their line is gone out through all the earth, and their words to the end of the world:
In them hath he set a tabernacle for the Sunne.

We doubt.

Breathing the breath of life into every living thing.
Causing the bud of the tender herb to spring forth.
Finding the place of understanding.

A few days ago. The late afternoon sun begins to cool.
The fields where I kept my camels. The surviving servant showing me over the site.
Explaining how it happened. How it took them all by surprise. How all of them were on guard. Watching the paths and watching the fields. The Chaldeans made three bands! They were stealthy! We were caught by surprise! They fell among the camels! They carried them away! Your faithful servants made resistance! Every one of them was slain with the edge of the sword! I only managed to escape and come to tell thee! There are scuff marks in the soil. Stark signs of a major brawl. The women cry and the children wail. The bodies of my servants wrapped in linen. A horn sounds from the rise of the hill. A messenger is coming, Master! I can barely make him out! It looks like a household servant of your eldest son!

An elder brother spoke in jest to his younger brother.
My inheritance to you for a mess of pottage.
I will put my word in writing – in the snow.

"Thy sons and thy daughters were eating and drinking wine in their eldest brother's house! And there came a great wind from the wilderness, and smote the four corners of the house, and it fell upon the young men and they are dead! I only am escaped alone to tell thee!"

Look a gift mule in the mouth - better to talk - he commanded, and it stood fast - like the waves of the sea - I have been young, and now i am old - manifests his innate superiority - he contemplated chaos - questions i want to ask - giveth and taketh away - your needs will not be ignored.

Opening the huge doors of God's palace! There are many, many things that I would like to know! Why are people able to make children? Why does the sun keep people warm? Why do the stars guide our wanderings? Why does a rainbow follow a storm? Is all of this planned or does it just happen? I am almost in his presence! Perhaps if I shout he will be able to hear! You could have made things perfect! You could have made a perfect world! Why did you not make earth like heaven? I shout and shout but I hear no answer! Is there no one present to hear? What is the reason for the creation of humankind?

A man with a son. A man with a precious son. Under the heavy burden of an edict from his god.

A young shepherd haunting the sales of the neighbouring lands.
A traveller trapped on a ledge.
A young man questioning visitors at a well.

A donkey. Two servants. Wood and coals and a knife.

Which is as a bridegrome comming out of his chamber, and reioyceth as a strong man to runne a race.
 His going forth is from the end of the heauen, and his circuite vnto the ends of it: and there is nothing hidde from the heat thereof.

The son asking questions. The father deep in thought. Walking along with his precious son on the way to a sacrifice.

Do you dream about your children?
Do they live and breathe in your thoughts?
Are they more alive to you than the people you see?

We affirm.

Standing in the throne room of heaven! There is no one here! A gigantic room with a marble floor and a long carpet sweeping from the huge doors up to the foot of the throne! A gigantic throne made of marble which sits up high on a dias! Not a guard, not an angel, not a messenger! No sign of anyone or anything! No one waiting for God to appear! Will I be first to have questions answered? How long should I wait for God? Perhaps there will not be an audience! Where would he be instead of here? I have so many questions that I want to ask when he appears! I do not find him on the earth! I do not find him here in heaven! Where can he be?

Chapter 3

Alone on the ash-heap.
A woman who shares ten children with her husband.

Agonizing boils. Boils from the sole of my foot to my crown. My whole body wracked with pain. If I sit, I want to stand. If I stand, I want to sit down. Every bone of my body aches. My skin is pocked with running sores. My eyes are filled with rheum. No one knows me by my looks. I shiver as I sit by the fire. I burn as I stand in the breeze. I am in agony every second. Every breath I take I hope will be my last.

My skin is on fire. My life is in ashes. My children are dead.

Man dieth and wasteth away. Man giveth up the ghost and where is he?

Five people sitting and talking on an ash-heap.
A land where all are welcome.
Two men who have not met for many years.

Man lieth down and riseth not. Till the heavens be no more, they shall not awake nor be raised out of their sleep.

Birthing lambs in the springtime.
Eating and drinking with my family.
Yoking the oxen for the plough.

A man's flesh knows only pain. His soul knows only mourning.

How do people react to such disasters?
What do they seem to think is the cause?
How have others reacted when such things have happened to them?

Alone on the ash-heap.
A woman who bears ten children in her womb.
I sit among the ashes. I scrape myself with a potsherd. Everything that I have valued has been destroyed. I sit here among the ashes and wonder why. I envy those who are dead. How merciful it would be to take my place with those who are no longer living. There the wicked cease from troubling. There the weary are at rest. There the prisoners rest together. They hear not the voice of the oppressor. The small and the great are there and the servant is free from his master. God owes me a death. If only God would send my death to me.

God is our maker.
He giveth songs in the night.

We flourish.

A man staggers along in the desert sun.
Extreme exhaustion, parching thirst, intense heat.
A large bird circles slowly overhead.

On the night of my return. Lanterns in the courtyard of my house.
The wife of all my children. Everything she lives for. Everything that matters in her life.
It is early for my return. The servants are working in the courtyard. One of them rushes inside to announce my arrival. A cry from inside the house. My wife comes running out to meet me. She knows before I tell her. She senses evil in the air. She comes towards me with her face stricken with horror. What has brought you back so soon? What has been happening while you were gone? Why is your face so devastated? Your clothes are torn and your eyes have been weeping! Why do you mourn? She crumples down in the dust as I tell her the news.

Fire-pit near our dwelling - i will incline mine ear to a parable - pocked with running sores - chatting cheerfully in the marketplace - have to make a decision - these reasons seem conclusive - the weary are at rest - from the end of the earth i will cry unto thee - a kind of freedom and ability to bear his fate - we mourn, we doubt, we lose.

"The greatest man in the land of Uz! The man who is always perfect and upright! The one who fears God and eschewes evil! Camels, oxen, sheep! The greatest of all the men of the East! None like him in the earth! A perfect and upright man! Where is the hedge that you said was about you? Where is the hedge about thy house? Where is the hedge that you said was about you on every side? Seven sons and three daughters! Where are my sons?

Where are my daughters? Answer me that! And dost thou still retain thine integrity? Curse God and die!"

In thee, O Lord, doe I put my trust, let me neuer be put to confusion.
Deliuer mee in thy righteousnesse, and cause me to escape: incline thine eare vnto me, and saue me.

Alone on the ash-heap.
A woman who suckles her children at her breast.
Why did the wind come out of the wilderness? Why did the house collapse on that day? Why did not one of them escape to return to comfort their mother? I had sanctified my children. It was early in the day. I gave burnt offerings according to the number of them all. It might be, I thought, that my sons have sinned and cursed God in their hearts. I wanted to put them right with God on that day. What did they do that brought their destruction? They were wonderful in my sight. Mattan, Jemima, Heber, Epher, Bazak, Kezia, Evron, Avram, Noach, Keren. All of them happy, all of them healthy, all of them pious, in their way. The young are never as strict as their elders, of course, but surely God would know what is in the hearts of those whose lives are filled with the distractions of the day. Surely God knows how pure in heart my children were.

God thundreth marvellously with his voice.
Great things doth he which we cannot comprehend.

We falter.

A camel looked a donkey in the eye.
I contribute more than you to life on the earth.
When I have time I am going to make a list.

Zophar and I. When we were young and sharing our dreams.
I am strolling alone through the market-place. In the land of the Naamathites. Observing the sheep in their pens. Tempted to envy those who have money enough to buy.
I could afford a few sheep, or course, perhaps a dozen or so, but where would I graze my sheep in the summertime? In summer, the meadows near my house are scorched and bare. I only have a few fields and I raise camels and donkeys, but sheep are hard on the fields and I have no lush land. I speak to Zophar, the Naamathite, a fellow of about my age. He has brought some sheep to market that he wishes to sell. Come buy my sheep, my friend. You will not regret it. I will sell you the finest ewes and the boldest rams. They will produce the finest offspring. In no time at all, you will have the finest herds. You are Job, are you not, from the land of Uz? Why do you haunt the sheep markets in all the surrounding lands and

not buy a thing? Your herds must be large and splendid if the offerings of such as myself are beneath your standards. Take this ram, here, in my pen. He will sell within the hour. You had better buy him quickly or you will lose him. Can your flocks boast a more splendid beast than this?

> *Making a decree for the rain.*
> *Delivering the poor that cry.*
> *Multiplying my days in the sand.*

"Buy some of my sheep and I will help you. I will help you become established. I will allow you to use my meadow to build up your flock."

"A very generous offer, Zophar. I would be bound to you for life. This is more than I would expect from my closest friend."

"There is plenty of grass on my hillside. Our flocks could graze side by side. If you promise that in future you will buy all your sheep from me."

> Does God take care of children in danger?
> Does he see each sparrow fall?
> Is that his concern?

Alone on the ash-heap.
A woman who washes their bodies and combs their hair.
If only I had been with them. I was drinking at the well. It was early in the morning. They were gathering at the house to have a feast. All of my sons together. And they had sent for their three sisters to eat and drink with them. I was on my way to my fields. I was making my usual rounds. The inspection of my holdings. Checking the folds and the pens. The message came from my eldest son. An invitation to attend. I wish that I had dropped everything and rode to my eldest son's house. I would gladly have perished with them. Let the roof fall on me as well. My only regret would be leaving my wife behind.

A wadi is never the same. It is life when rain is plenty. It is death when the rains are withheld.

> *And God said, Let there be light: and there was light.*

Dreams torment me when I doze for a few moments. Did I ever used to dream? I don't remember.

Alone on the ash-heap.
A woman who cooks their breakfast and teaches their sums.

My wife comes to see me every day. She brings a bowl of food and a jug of water. She seldom says a word. In my turn, I seldom speak to her. What is one to say? She has no one who can comfort her. Her sisters offer her comfort but she asks them to leave. What are her sisters' children to her? Is God mocking her in her grief? Her sisters always come for the largest feasts. But for whom are they to prepare a feast today? A bowl of food and a flask of water is all I need. And the taste thereof is bitter in my mouth. Her sisters' presence is a reminder to her of the days when her children were alive. We would roast oxen in the courtyard. We would burn offerings in honour of our God. All of the children would gather around and we elders would tell them stories. And always we would begin and end with a prayer.

Thou shalt come to thy grave in a full age.
Like a shock of corn cometh in his season.

We gain.

A mule and a human rode along.
If mules were human said the mule,
We would generously have our mules carry half the load.
If only God would hear and make this change.

Many years ago. I am a growing boy.
I am sitting around a campfire in our village, near the well.
My mother's father is telling stories. His brothers and his sisters and all of their children are present as well. My grandfather starts with a story and then the others take their turns. From the eldest to the youngest sibling of that generation, and only the males. Children are not allowed to talk, as they have only lived in the village and have nothing to offer. Women would have only tales of sewing or of cooking the food. The tales are of camels crossing deserts, of dry wells and arid streams, of blinding sandstorms and trickling oases and shading palms. My grandfather – my mother's father – takes his turn, once again, after the other males have spoken, and his stories always seem the best to me. He rolls up his sleeves and shows the scars. The scar-tissue gleams in the glow of the fire. The blade of a sword! It bled for days! I rode my camel for mile after mile! I left a trail of blood-drops in the sand! I never thought I would see my wife and children ever again! The brigands had left me there for dead! They mistook your tough old grandfather for a lesser man! My camel had run away or they would have taken it as well! I knew where it would be and I followed it there!

Stroke him under the chin - these doctrines afford no satisfaction - contribute more than you - unto thee shall all flesh come - hope that god is in a good mood - i was shocked -

see each sparrow fall - i cried unto god with my voice - has become an insoluble riddle - he trusted on the lord.

"For as far back as time has been remembered, our family has gone out on the caravans. It is an honourable way of life. The time has arrived for young Job to travel too."

"Young Job is not much more than a boy. Are you sure that he is old enough? Camels are very dangerous beasts and he is quite young."

"He is old enough to begin to earn his keep. He will go out on the caravans with the men. We will take him with us after the seasonal rains."

A crippling of plans by a major setback.
A man carrying washing from a lagoon.
Nicks on the ears of young lambs.

Alone on the ash-heap.
A woman who loses her children to a great wind.
The greatest man in the land of Uz. The man who was known as Job. The man who was perfect and upright. The man who feared God and eschewed evil. It took me years to build up my household. I stuck to the rules at every turn. There were many shady dealings all around me. Not an enterprise that didn't offer a means of cheating. I was Job, the man you could trust. I was the man whose hand was his bond. An embrace was all that was needed. Whole herds were exchanged on my say-so. Whole caravans braved the desert because of my word. I was known to be God-protected. The man whose partner was the Almighty. Every agreement was guaranteed. Every night I would look at the stars and renew my bargain. Every morning I would look at the sun and thank my God. God and I in a perfect union. Sharers in every enterprise. None like me in the earth. A perfect and upright man. A man that feareth God and escheweth evil.

O God, be not farre from mee: O my God, make haste for my helpe.
But I wil hope continually, and will yet praise thee more and more.

We lose.

Fearing God and eschewing evil.
Listening to advice.
Mourning a great loss.

My wife and I at the ash-heap. Her sisters and their children gathered round. Not one of her own children is left to comfort her in her grief.

The wife of all my children. Her cheeks wet with weeping. Clothing rent and ashes in her hair.

What am I to say to her? What can I possibly say? She has lost everything that mattered. She has lost all that she had to live for. She bore them in her womb and suckled them at her breast. She washed their bodies and combed their hair and fed them their breakfast and taught them their sums. She held them on her knees and dried their tears. All swept away in an instant. All gone as if in a flood. The sheep, the goats, the oxen, meant nothing to her at all. Every thought that she had – waking in the morning, settling down to sleep at night – was for God and her brood.

> *A group of clouds gathered over a dry wadi.*
> *It always seemed to happen without fail.*
> *Rains fell, flowers grew, the desert bloomed.*
> *No human moved along the desert trail.*

"Thou speakest as one of the foolish women speaketh. What? Shall we receive good at the hand of God, and shall we not receive evil? I am ashamed to hear a wife of mine say such things. I have never sinned with my lips. I shall not do so now. I will scrape myself with a potsherd. I will sit among the ashes. And I will contemplate why this evil has come upon us."

> *Feare was on every side - what you had to say - dry wells and arid streams - the origin of evil is not explained - fowl of the air, fish of the sea - wilt thou be angry forever - known to be god-protected - it is uncertain what is meant - the best-possible job - with honey out of the rock.*

Alone on the ash-heap.
A woman with rent clothing and ashes in her hair.
Rewarded beyond belief. Seven thousand sheep. Three thousand camels. Five hundred yoke of oxen. Five hundred she-asses. A very great household. The greatest of all the men of the East. A man with a hedge about him. A hedge about his house. A hedge about all that he had on every side. God had blessed the work of his hands. His substance increased in the land. The man upon whose shoulder was the hand of God.

An old man who is now blind. An old man at the end of his life. An old man with trembling hands and failing eyes.

> *A girl with a dress of colourful patches.*
> *Pregnant ewes grazing on a hillside.*
> *A circle of camel drivers discussing the route.*

An old man with two sons. An old man with a blessing to give. An old man who has lived his life in service to his god.

O God, thou hast taught me from my youth: and hitherto haue I declared thy wonderous workes.
Now also when I am old and gray headed, O God, forsake me not: vntill I haue shewed thy strength vnto this generation, and thy power to euery one that is to come.

Calling his first-born son before him. Telling his son that his aged father will soon die. Arranging for his blessing in its proper time.

My wife has sent word to Barachel, my oldest and most trusted friend.
Why has he not arrived? Why has he not sent word?
Surely something is wrong. He would brave the desert for me if he was able.

What do you say to other people?
What advice do they give to you?
Are words and thoughts inadequate at a time like this?

We endure.

Alone on the ash-heap.
A woman who advises her husband to curse God and die.
God has considered his servant Job. God has put forth his hand. God has touched all that I have. God has cursed me to my face. All of my children gone in an instant. A slap in the face from my God. My wife a living shadow. Devastated by her loss. She has nothing left to live for. Nothing to do except to weep. To bring me, once a day, a bowl of food and a jug of water. To this she has been reduced by the wrath of God.

Chapter 4

I am the best-possible Job! I am in the days of my prime! I am sitting in my home! My children are all about me! Every one! Mattan, Jemima, Heber, Epher, Bazak, Kezia, Evron, Avram, Noach, Keren! My wife is by my side! We bow our heads before a table which groans with food! This is the goodness that God provides! These are the blessings for which we give thanks! A family around a table thanking God! God has blessed and continues blessing! His kindness increases daily! God and man in perfect harmony on this earth! My table is overloaded! I can think of nothing more that the Lord could give!

There is hope for a tree, if it be cut down. It will sprout again and the tender branch thereof will not cease.

Friends coming to visit in an hour of need.
A young man whose trade might be a brigand.
A man who repents in dust and ashes.

Though the root grows old in the earth. Though the stock dies in the ground.

Feeling my glory fresh in me.
Saying to a king thou art wicked.
Knowing all the works of men.

With the scent of water, it will bud. It will bring forth boughs like a plant.

Can you say that you have been your best-possible self?
That you have done as you should have done?
That you have not done what you should not have done?

I am the best-possible Job! I am in the days of my prime! I am standing in one of my fields! I am talking to my overseer! He is telling me that the grain is not as fullsome as it has been in other years! He has held the gleaners back! He wants to sweep the field again, to try to increase the yield to the level which we have achieved in other years! I look at the poor who stand waiting at the edge of my field! Their woven baskets in their hands, dangling at their sides in a sign of despair! Let them glean, I say to my overseer! They are poor and I am wealthy! My family is well fed and God has been good! I wave my arm and invite the poor to glean my field!

Thou shalt be hid from the scourge of the tongue.
Neither shalt thou be afraid of destruction when it cometh.

We hope.

Double to win. Double to win.
This is my motto. Double to win.
Would you live all your life on the head of a pin?
This is my motto. Double to win.

Four of us on the ash-heap. Three acquaintances have arrived. Elphaz, Bildad, and Zophar. A Temanite, a Shuhite and a Naamathite.

A long journey over difficult terrain. Friends and rivals over the course of many years.

They stare at me in wonder. They do not know me. My skin is running sores. Have they not heard about the boils? Why have they come to see me? Who was it who informed them of my plight? We have been business rivals and partners. We built our herds, our wealth, our prestige, in competition and in conflict. Do they come as comforters or accusers? Do they wish to put me right with the Almighty or to demonstrate to God that they are right with him and that I am worse than they? They sit in a circle beside me. They tear their mantles and weep their tears. They sprinkle dust from the ash-heap on top of their heads and they pray.

Suffering through a sandstorm - lower than the angels - walk in darkness - to oppose men in their pretensions - a god full of compassion - the days of my prime - the work of thy fingers - the inexplicable blows of fate - a traveller trapped on a ledge - of old hast thou laid the foundation of the earth.

We sit in silence. We do not speak. We say no words.

Haue mercy vpon me, O Lord, for I am in trouble; mine eie is consumed with griefe, yea my soule and my belly.

For my life is spent with griefe, and my yeeres with sighing: my strength faileth, because of mine iniquitie, and my bones are consumed.

I am the best-possible Job! I am in the days of my prime! I sit inside the house of a widow! I am sitting on the dirt floor! Her children cling to her robes! She is weeping silently! I am sorry to lose a good man! Your husband was faithful to me for many years! I have known him from a boy! He tended my sheep as if he was tending those of his own! Many a lamb has survived because your husband had the care! I cannot restore your husband, but I can assure you that your needs will not be ignored! I pledge to you and to your children that you shall eat and drink in this house as if your husband had still been present and you in his care! This shall be true until your children come of age!

God sets an end to darkness.
He searches out all perfection.

We fear.

A tree grew in the forest.
It stretched its roots towards the centre of the earth.
But it never got there.

Many years ago. When Eliphaz and I were both young men.

Examining a mule. Examining his hoofs. Examining his teeth. Looking for tell-tale signs that lurk in the eyes. A mule who is highly praised by Eliphaz.

Over the years, I build up my holdings. My fields, my crops, my herds. I make my plans and keep them secret. Not even to Eliphaz, my friend, do I tell my plans. I am building up my holdings in order to be able to approach Baruch, the trader from the land of Tirzah, six days away by caravan, to ask for his eldest daughter's hand. I have never spoken to her since that day at the well. I have never told Baruch of my intentions. I do everything in order. Time needs to ripen like everything else. All things will work together as best they may. Eliphaz and I are friends, certain enough, but we are also rivals. Over the years we spend time together, whether in his land or in mine. We buy and sell at each other's markets – he on a visit to the land of Uz; me on a visit to the land of the Temanites. If I buy a bull, in order to bulk my herd, it won't be long before Eliphaz will buy a bigger bull. If I tell him that I now have twenty donkeys, before next visit he will count his herd and will find he has more. When we trade, I am very wary. Eliphaz always teases me. Job my friend, do you not know the old adage! It has, no doubt, come down to us from ancient times! Never look a gift mule in the mouth! A beast for sale is not a gift, my dear friend, Eliphaz. You want your fair share in return, do you not? Surely you can't be in such a big hurry. Let me take my time with this trade. Surely you only want to obtain from it that which is fair. Eliphaz teases me about everything. Eliphaz needles endlessly. What about this? What about that? What about such another thing? He is always asking me questions. He wants to know my every thought. About my crops, about my weather, about trading at the market, about my past, about my present, about my future.

> *Watching the sun go down.*
> *Ploughing in the spring-time.*
> *Feasting with our family in our house.*

"You will soon be looking for a wife, Job, my friend. I wonder who it shall be. You are at the stage where starting a family should be a concern."

"I am not ready yet, my friend. I am building up my holdings. I believe in doing things in a rational way."

"You would do well to consider it seriously. The eldest daughter of Baruch would make a fine wife. Do you remember when we met her at the well?"

> Have you always given the best of yourself in every relationship?
> Have you always assumed the best in all of your friends?
> Have you harboured secret envy or unfounded rage?

I am the best-possible Job! I am in the days of my prime! I stand in front of a hut in a remote ravine! A young farmer stands beside me, a man of my employ! I have overheard some talk and have learned that he is troubled! An older man comes to the door! I take him by the collar and give him a shake! You have sold a goat to this man! You have taken his wages from him! The goat was defective and you must have known it to be so! Go inside and get the coins and bring them forward! You must make a restitution and an apology! God is watching your every transaction! You must do penance and hope that God is in a good mood! I take pity on your wife and children! Do these things and you shall remain in my employ!

The mountains are always there. They are as old as the earth itself. They form a background to the life that we live each day.

> *And God said, Let the waters vnder the heauen be gathered together vnto one place, and let the dry land appeare: and it was so.*

If I ever used to dream, these dreams must have been peaceful and soothing and gorgeous. I must have dreamed of water trickling down from the melting of mountain snows and the dancing of rivulets through green pastures with flocks of pregnant ewes grazing on the hillsides. And when I awoke, I must have yawned beside my door and climbed on my little donkey and ridden towards my fields, or pushed the flap of my tent open and stretched my arms and looked around at my mountain-fed rivulets and my fields of green grasses and my ewes.

If I had dreams, they were as pleasant to me as my days.

I am the best-possible Job! I am in the days of my prime! I stand beside the village lagoon! The blind and lame are all around me! One by one, I take their hands and lead them down the slope and into the water! I hold their hands and talk to them and splash the healing water on their bodies! When they are ready, I help them up the slope again! I have my attendant give them a towel to dry them off! Then I repeat the process again! The waters are soothing to the afflicted! They are balm to a mind in pain! I always make time to take my place at the village lagoon! It is my gift to the blind and the lame! It is my way of remaining humble! It is my way of saying there but for God go I!

The triumph of the wicked is short.
The joy of the hypocrite but for a moment.

We rejoice.

You say that you want to talk, my wife.
Though silence was golden before.
It is words that leave the deepest wounds.
I would rather you use a knife.

Many years ago. When I was coming to manhood.

The first rays of dawn. Savouring the first breath of fresh air on the opening of the tent-flap.

My father and my mother and all of our siblings. On the hillside in the spring. Green grass and gentle rains have carpeted the meadow with colourful flowers. I come to the fire with an arm-load of kindling and my father, as soon as the fire is hot enough for my mother, takes me aside. Job, my son, you have come to an age when you will have to make a decision. Our village lies in a place where there is desert and there are hills. Your mother's father's people have always gone out on the caravans. They have faced the desert boldly, through sandstorms and other strife, in order to fetch the goods that are found in other lands. You have spent much time with these people and know their ways. My father's people have always been those who have raised and tended the flocks. You have spent time with them and know the risks and rewards. I want you to consider carefully, Job. Which way of life appeals to you? You have my word that I will honour your choice. We stand in the grass of the mountain-side meadow and look out over the desert, where a small caravan wends its way along.

Marvellous things without number - i will sing unto the lord as long as i live - from ancient times - a polydaemonistic stage of religion - the deepest wounds - flocks of pregnant ewes - here on the ground - all flesh shall perish together - the standing-ground of religion - they have ears, but they hear not.

"I have admired both ways of life, Father: that of the camel and that of the sheep."
"And?"
"I have been wondering, Father: why can I not have both?"

A blight which devastates the crops.
A woman suckling a child at her breast.
A father and a son mending a gate.

I am the best-possible Job! I am in the days of my prime! I am walking through my village! People bow as they see me come! I am the man whom God preserves! His candle shines upon my head and by his light I walk in darkness! The secret of God is in my tent! I am Job, the man who is perfect and upright! The man who fears God and eschewes evil! I have seven thousand sheep, three thousand camels and five hundred yoke of oxen! I have five hundred she-asses and a very great household! I am the greatest of all the great men of the East! God has shone his radiance upon me! The children of my loins number ten!

I was a reproch among all mine enemies, but especially among my neighbours, and a feare to mine acquaintance: they that did see me without, fled from me.
I am forgotten as a dead man out of minde: I am like a broken vessell.

We mourn.

Speaking with knowledge and with wisdom.
Making the weary to be at rest.
Commanding the eagle to mount up.

Four of us on the ash heap. Eliphaz, Bidad and Zophar sitting beside me.
Seven days and seven nights. A flask of water and a bowl of food. Nothing more.
Mourning beside me in silence. Never speaking a word. Dust on heads, torn mantles, furrowed brows. Why have they come to bother me? No doubt each of them wishes to speak to me. Their silence is a gift for which I am grateful. At least it allows me to think of other things.

A young shepherd was menaced by a fierce wolf.
He remembered the advice of his wise friend.
The young shepherd reached out and stroked the fierce wolf underneath the chin.
The wolf became placid. Almost a friend.

We sit in silence. We do not speak. We say no words.

My soul cleaveth unto the dust - silence was golden before - carpeted the meadow - pokes at the embers - this thou must do - thoughts raised to a higher power - risks and rewards - thou art my hiding place and my shield - the flies buzz on the ash-heap - god's mysterious invisibility.

I am the best-possible Job! I am in the days of my prime! I take my seat in the street! A place is made for me in the ring of elders who decide the questions of the community! Young men see me and hide from me! The aged arise and stand up as I arrive! Elders refrain from talking and lay their hands upon their mouths as I take my place! Chieftains hold their peace as if their tongues are cleaving to the roofs of their mouths! They know that their speeches are irrelevant! They know that the word of Job is as the law! Every ear is bent to hear the great Job speak!

A man in the glow of a burning bush. His sheep in disarray. His mind amazed.

A boy who calms disturbed animals with a wave of his hand.
Two men baring their souls as they travel a road.
A man who delivers a letter for a friend.

Listening to his god and making objections. What should I say? What should I think? What should I do?

For I haue heard the slaunder of many, feare was on euery side: while they tooke counsell together against me, they deuised to take away my life.
But I trusted in thee, O Lord: I sayd, Thou art my God.

Aware of his own misgivings. Aware of his own lack of skills. Astonished at the task which now is his.

There is still no word from Barachel, my oldest and most trusted friend.
I asked my wife to send word to him.
I wish that Barachel had come instead of these three.

Do you claim that you were the best-possible Job?
In the eyes of your fellows or in the eyes of your god?
What were the words that passed for wisdom each time you spoke?

We pray.

I am the best-possible Job! I am in the days of my prime! I am speaking in the village council! I sit in my place near the village gate! All eyes are on my person! All ears are given to me! They have waited for me to speak! Many have spoken, but all ears have waited to hear the great Job speak! They have waited for me as for rain! And now their mouths have opened wide for the rain that is the wisdom of my speech! I am Job! I sit in council! As a chief or a king at the head of an army! And all who hear my words take comfort from me!

Chapter 5

Four of us on the ash-heap.
A lone rider plodding along on a donkey.
Eliphaz is speaking. I barely listen. What does Eliphaz bring but words? Words of wisdom. Words of comfort. Words of praise for the Lord. Is there no one who can help me? I am hurting, Eliphaz, hurting. Did you bring no balm or oil for itching skin? I wish I could tear the skin from my bones and cast it aside.

My skin is on fire. My life is in ashes. My children are dead.

Oh that I knew where I might find God. That I might come even unto his presence.

Business, acquaintances, family left behind.
An irritated wife answering questions.
A man awaiting the arrival of an old friend.

I would order my cause before him. I would fill my mouth with arguments.

Suffering through a sand-storm.
Dwelling in a house of clay.
Gathering the vintage at harvest time.

I want to know the words by which he would answer me. I want to understand what he would say to me.

Have such disasters happened to others?
What have they thought when such things have occurred?
Did each of them think it could never have happened to them?

Four of us on the ash-heap.

A traveller trapped on a ledge with a broken leg.

Eliphaz is speaking. His words are wasted on me. My skin is a flaming furnace. Puss runs from my open sores. I wretch until I am empty. The food I eat is impossible to keep down. Eliphaz, I respect your right to speak, but I have questions that I would like to ask of you. Have I been brought unto the priest? Has the priest been to see me? Is the rising in my skin the colour of white? Has the hair of my skin turned white? Is there raw flesh rising in my skin?

The spirit of God hath made me.
The breath of the Almighty hath given me life.

We laugh.

A man and a camel in the desert.
Each senses a different path to the distant mountains.
Each looks at the other; neither blinks.
Am I the master here or are you?

Sitting in a circle on the ash-heap. Eliphaz, Bildad, Zophar and me. Seven days and nights and not a word.

Flies are buzzing. The heat is intense. The stench is fierce. In the distance, the gates of the town. The well where people gather to fetch their water and the gossip of the day. Caravans and merchants come and go.

Finally, after seven days and nights, I open my mouth and speak. I curse the day that I was born. The others listen politely and then Eliphaz, the Temanite, asks to be the first to speak in reply. I turn to him and I nod. My eyes are filled with rheum. My ears are plagued with buzzing. I strain to listen, but I am barely able to hear.

Perceiving the breadth of the earth - the sun comes up each morning - dwell in houses of clay - the lord that made heaven and earth - the constraint of the divine presence - delight in the almighty - a good and upright man - the god who tortures him - contribute more than you - oh lord, give ear unto my supplications.

"Shall mortal man be more just than God? Shall a man be more pure than his maker? Behold, he put no trust in his servants; and his angels he charged with folly. How much less in them that dwell in houses of clay, whose foundation is in the dust, which are crushed before the moth? Although affliction cometh not forth of the dust, neither doth trouble spring out of the ground. Yet man is born unto trouble, as the sparks fly upward. I would seek unto God, and unto God would I commit my cause. Which doeth great things and unsearchable; marvellous things without number. Who giveth rain upon the earth, and sendeth waters upon the fields. To set up on high those that be low; that those which mourn may be exalted to safety. Behold, happy is the man whom God correcteth, therefore despise not thou the chastening of the Almighty. For he maketh sore, and bindeth up. He woundeth and his hands make whole. Lo this, we have searched it, so it is. Hear it and know thou it for thy good."

     The Law of the Lord is perfect, conuerting the soule: the testimonie of the Lord is sure, making wise the simple.
     The Statutes of the Lord are right, reioycing the heart: the Commandement of the Lord is pure, inlightning the eyes.

    Four of us on the ash-heap.
    A man climbing a cliff with a man on his back.
    Eliphaz is speaking. How can I concentrate? Eliphaz. Oh Eliphaz. If only you would listen instead of talk. I have much that I want to ask you. There is much that I want to know. Has this happened in the land of the Temanites? Has anyone been a good and upright man – a man who has served God with every fibre of his being, a man who has been blessed and who has walked in the favour of the Lord – and then been struck down into the dirt as I have been?

    Hearken unto this.
    Stand still and consider the works of God.

    We cry.

    A man was alone on the desert.
    He cursed his vile luck.
    I am a lion, he said to himself.
    There are no people here for me to devour.

    Bildad and I as partners. Many years ago.
    At the well of my village, inside the town gate. Beggars seeking alms. Outfitters servicing travellers.
    Bildad has come here from the land of the Shuhites. A group of drivers readying our caravan. A caravan of mules. Each mule with two bulging sacks. Grain from Bildad's holdings. Grain from mine as well. Twenty-three donkeys for Bildad. Thirty-two donkeys for me. I have borrowed from my neighbours. A rare thing for me to do. I am gambling that my holdings will double and more. The extra money will be most welcome. Irrigation is the key. Rain is so rare that it is important to irrigate one's fields. A chance to build up my herds. Chiefly donkeys and camels at present. Later, when my wealth increases still more, I shall branch out into other endeavours. Of course, land is always the cornerstone. I must acquire

more land. I can almost taste the proceeds from this venture of ours. Bildad signals that all is in order. It is almost time to depart. He turns his back on me. He readies the straws in his hand for me to draw.

> *Cutting out rivers among rocks.*
> *Causing the widow's heart to sing for joy.*
> *Being father to the poor.*

"The luck is with you, my friend! You need only remain behind and oversee our holdings! I must suffer the dusty trail for a trek of two weeks!"

"Luck is not a factor. Caution is the key. You must be cautious at every stage of this venture, my friend."

"We will more than double our profits! These people are desperate for foreign grain! After this venture, both of our futures will be assured!"

> Why do we all not live long and peacefully?
> All of us living our lives to the full?
> No diseases or disasters to take us away?

> Four of us on the ash-heap.
> *A heap of bones on a canyon floor.*

Eliphaz is speaking. Why should I bother to listen? Ten children, Eliphaz. Has this happened in the land of the Temanites? Seven of them men and three of them girls. My wife has been struck a blow. A withering blast from the Almighty. Our support in our old age. Has anyone in your homeland been treated so? Oh, you drone and drone and drone. Can you tell me what the priest has said? Is my plague spread in my garment? Has my garment been burnt by the priest? Have my clothes been burnt in the fire? Is my plague a fretting leprosy? Am I unclean?

The desert sands are always shifting. Flat and inviting and stretching for miles. A highway for the caravans that trade.

> *And God called the drie land, Earth, and the gathering together of the waters called hee, Seas: and God saw that it was good.*

A little boy brings food. A bowl of scraps for us to share and a small jug of cold water to whet our thirst.

He never says a word. Perhaps an adult finger has been raised to adult lips. Do not speak to the men on the ash-heap.

But who has sent him here? Or does he come with food and water on his own?

Four of us on the ash-heap.
A man, a donkey and an invalid plodding along.
Eliphaz is speaking! Was there ever more waste of words? He has insisted on giving a speech. It is agony to listen. What can he possibly say to me? Oh why was my hearing not taken away?

All flesh shall perish together.
Man shall turn again into dust.

We wonder.

A cobbler sells his sandals in the marketplace.
All admire the sandals that he displays.
Splendid caravans arrive from far-away lands.
Princes, kings and potentates clamour to buy.

Will my problems never cease?
A load of grain on a granary floor.
Who has done this, I ask my men. How could anyone be so foolish as to dump a load of grain on a granary floor? The floor is rock. The grain is dry. There will be moisture seep up through the rock and the grain will be dampened and the fungus will grow and soon all of the grain will rot and spoil. You might as well have dumped the grain on the ash-heap at the edge of the village and set it afire. The men are silent awhile, and look down at their feet. Then one of them, Old Seth, ventures to speak. The grain was in a cart, Master. It was left here out of the rain as the darkness fell. Then, this morning, as we were waiting for the baskets to arrive so we could unload the grain from the cart, your first-born son came here in a hurry. He said that he needed a cart to move some furniture for the mother of his wife and was short of time. He ordered us to dump the grain on the granary floor. But did none among you explain that the grain would rot? The same hesitation. He said he was in a hurry, Master. He is the first-born son. He has shown his ire before. He does not encourage discussion when he gives an order. We thought it best to act upon his word. All right men, you acted on orders. Let that be an end of it. I see the baskets have arrived. This happened not so long ago. Please collect the grain in baskets while it is still dry. I will speak to my son and prevent this from happening again. There will be bonuses for those who do this for me. It is Mattan, my first-born son. He means well, but is lacking in judgement. He yearns for authority with the men. He no longer wishes to see himself as a boy. All of this I rehearse with my wife at the end of the day.

We rejoice, we wonder, we gain - a withering blast from the almighty - I meditate on all thy works - she has found a way - the primeval monsters of chaos - does not encourage discussion - children chant lustily - holding the soul of every living thing - that our garners may be full - to maintain his consciousness of innocence.

"I must think of what to say. I must phrase it very carefully. Some prerogatives should be his and some should not."

"Why do you hesitate? Just tell him. Grain when left on rock will be sure to rot."

"It is not so simple as that. He is chafing at the bit. How to tell him that Father and First-born are not in a race?"

Two young men who are sharing their dreams.
A man shaking dirt and ashes from a ragged robe.
Hunters hardening their spears in a fire.

Four of us on the ash-heap.
A man with a grip on the handle of a knife.
Eliphaz is speaking. I barely listen. I barely hear. None of my sons was named Eliphaz. None of my sons was named Bildad or Zophar. And all with good reason. There was a day when I would have gladly taken each of these names as the name of my first-born son. Well, friendship fades like sheep-dye. Good friends are hard to find and harder to keep. Sheep, camels, donkeys, all respond predictably to nurturing, but friendships often develop in disturbing ways.

The feare of the Lord is cleane, enduring for euer: the Iudgements of the Lord are true, and righteous altogether.

More to bee desired are they then gold, yea, then much fine gold: sweeter also then hony, and the hony combe.

We doubt.

Listening to the braying of the ass.
Gathering scraps of wisdom.
Complaining in the bitterness of my soul.

The four of us in a circle. Sitting on the ash-heap. I am expected to offer Eliphaz a reply.

Flies buzz. The sun is fierce. My throat is dry.

The words of Eliphaz are many. He seems to have so much to say. He has been waiting seven days and seven nights to deliver his wisdom. What can I say to Eliphaz? That there is nothing in what he says? That I would speak with God or speak with no one at all? I swallow my spittle. I attempt to clear my throat. I raise the flask to my lips in vain. Where is my wife? Where is the boy? How to answer Eliphaz? What can I say?

An elder brother spoke in jest to his younger brother.
My inheritance to you for a mess of pottage.
I will put my word in writing – in the sand.

"Oh that I might have my request and that God would grant me the thing that I long for! Even that it would please God to destroy me. That he would let loose his hand, and cut me off. What is my strength, that I should hope? And what is mine end, that I should prolong my life? Is my strength the strength of stones? Or is my flesh of brass? Teach me, and I will hold my tongue: and cause me to understand wherein I have erred. When I lie down, I say, When shall I arise, and the night be gone? And I am full of tossings to and fro unto the dawning of the day. My flesh is clothed with worms and clods of dust. My skin is broken and become loathsome. My days are swifter than a weaver's shuttle and are spent without hope. I will not refrain my mouth; I will speak in the anguish of my spirit; I will complain in the bitterness of my soul. What is man, that thou shouldest magnify him? And that thou shouldest set thine heart upon him? And that thou shouldest visit him every morning and try him every moment? Why hast thou set me as a mark against thee, so that I am a burden to myself? And why dost thou not pardon my transgression and take away mine iniquity? For now shall I sleep in the dust; and thou shalt seek me in the morning, but I shall not be."

Being together is a blessing - which of his sons is he - the paths of the seas - fades like sheep-dye - resolve to speak without fear - to understand my deepest concerns - put not your trust in princes - more to bee desired - a conception which spreads its branches wide - he telleth the number of the stars.

Four of us on the ash-heap.
Two men embracing in a gesture of friendship.
Eliphaz is speaking. Oh why do I still have my ears? Why have these friends come here to see me? Do they not have ash-heaps in their villages? Are there no sufferers near their homes? Why are they offering me vacuous wisdom? Why not keep it to themselves? Do they think that God will think well of them if they tell me how wrong I have been? What is he saying? What will I answer? I try to listen closely but my mind constantly wanders to other things.

A man walking along. His precious son by his side. Deep in thought.

Young girls laughing and chirping in the sunshine.

A friend sending word of the birth of a first-born son.
Camels plodding along in single file.

Remembering the words of his god. This thou must do. This I must have.

Moreouer by them is thy seruant warned: and in keeping of them there is great reward.
Who can vnderstand his errours? cleanse thou me from secret faults.

Go to the mountain. Build a pyre. Make a sacrifice.

A lone rider on a fine horse comes through the gate. Not Barachel, my friend for life, but his first-born son.

The flies buzz on the ash-heap. The sun beats down on the village.

"My name is Elihu, son of Barachel, the Buzite, of the kindred of the Ram. My father is unwell. He would have come, as soon as he heard, but he is ill and in a raging fever. He has sent me, his first-born son, in his place. I pleaded to be let to stay, but my father insisted. My father cautioned me not to speak. 'You are young, my first-born son. Attend to my true friend, Job, but show forth your presence only, as representing your father, and not yourself. Do not speak, even if asked, as your words would not convey the sound of my voice.'"

Why would God want life to end early?
Would he not want us to live our full span?
Hasn't the deaths of your children altered what would seem to be God's plan?

We affirm.

Five of us on the ash-heap.
A man with a finger on his lips.
My friend, Barachel, is ailing. I am sure that he is near to death. He and I are as close as brothers. If he was able, he would have come to me, as I would have gone to him if he had sent word. I feel a great sense of relief. My friend, Barachel, has responded. His presence here is in the person of his eldest son.

Chapter 6

I am the worst-possible Job! I am Job, the self-made man! The most important man in the land of Uz! Everything that I have I have made on my own! I have seven thousand sheep, three thousand camels and five hundred yoke of oxen! I have five hundred she-asses and a very great household! I am the greatest among the great men of the East! I have built my house with my own two hands! God has had nothing to do with my prosperity!

The wicked live, become old and are mighty in power.

A young man buying sheep from a new friend.
A young boy gathering firewood.
A tent on the hillside in the spring.

Their seed is established in their sight and their offspring prosper before their eyes.

Delivering men from going down to the pit.
Enlightening with the light of the living.
Perceiving the breadth of the earth.

Their houses are safe from fear, and the rod of God is not laid upon them.

What would you be if you were the worst-possible Job?
Is it possible that you have been this man all along?
Is this what your friends' speeches are designed to prove?

I am the worst-possible Job! I am Job, the self-made man! A young girl from another village! The girl who helps my wife with the household chores! The bother of petty requests! My wife has taken pity and it is up to me to be firm for both of us! The girl says that her mother is dying, but how do we know? Was it not her grandmother that drew her away before?

She is homesick, nothing more! She has found a way – with the story of the illness of her grandmother – to get to go home and visit her family every so often! She has marked you out for a weak one! One who tears up at every lie! Tell the girl she must do her duty! She is lucky to have her place! Tell her that the master says that if there is any more whining about her family she will be sent away for good!

The joy of the hypocrite is but for a moment.
He shall perish forever like his own dung.

We flourish.

A man staggers into a wadi.
He scatters the rocks and scratches at the ground.
Not a single drop of moisture to quench his thirst.

Five of us on the ash-heap. Beside me sits Elihu, the son of my old friend, Barachel.

Covered in soot and ashes. One of us in mourning and four in sympathy. Sympathy for something they cannot know or understand.

Bildad wishes to speak. Why should I listen? He has asked to follow Eliphaz. Why do friends seek to badger me with advice? I have no wish to hear people talk. Against my better judgement, I nod to him.

Kind to come to my side - cannot find him out - done this on my own - young men and maidens; old men and children - the problem of evil - break my silence - like his own dung - to test goodness that may be only skin-deep - message that you might wish to send - let them praise his name in the dance.

"How long wilt thou speak these things? And how long shall the words of thy mouth be like a strong wind? Doth God pervert judgment? Or doth the Almighty pervert justice? If thy children have sinned against him and he have cast them away for their transgression; if thou wouldest seek unto God betimes and make thy supplication to the Almighty; if thou wert pure and upright, surely now he would awake for thee and make the habitation of thy righteousness prosperous. Though thy beginning was small, yet thy latter end should greatly increase. Can the rush grow up without mire? Can the flag grow without water? Whilst it is yet in his greenness, and not cut down, it withereth before any other herb. So are the paths of all that forget God. The hypocrite's hope shall perish, whose hope shall be cut off, and whose trust shall be a spider's web. He shall lean upon his house, but it shall not stand. He shall hold it fast, but it shall not endure. He is green before the sun, and his branch shooteth forth in his garden. His roots are wrapped about the heap, and seeth the place of stones. Behold, this is the joy of his way, and out of the earth shall others grow. Behold, God will not cast away a perfect man, neither will he help the evil doers, till he fill thy mouth with laughing and thy lips with rejoicing."

My soule, wait thou onely vpon God: for my expectation is from him.
He onely is my rocke and my saluation; he is my defence; I shall not bee moued.

I am the worst-possible Job! I am Job, the self-made man! I am bustling through the village! The lame and the blind at the village well! They sit on the ground and wait for others to come and help them! It is good that people help them, but I decided long ago that I could never build up my herds and my flocks and my fields if I spent my time in helping the halt and the lame! I have no time to spend at the pool in idle chatter and charitable acts! The lame look my way as I approach the pool! The blind have no way of knowing that I am near! My time is gold to me; I have not one nugget to spare! I look the other way as I hurry past!

God cutteth out rivers among the rocks.
His eye seeth every precious thing.

We falter.

A goat looked a sheep in the eye.
I contribute more than you to life on the earth.
When I have time I am going to make a list.

Zophar and I. When we were young and sharing our dreams.
At Zophar's meadow on the hillside. Tiny rivulets trickling down among the rocks and green grass waving in the breezes that flow from the mountain.
It is my dream come true at last. Not my meadow, not my stream, not my breezes from the mountain. But still, due to the generosity of my good friend, Zophar, I shall at last have my flock. And soon, many flocks. It is the beginning of a great and glorious enterprise. My sheep are grazing on the hillside. Each mouthful of grass is a coin in my purse. Each grazer is building up my holdings and each one is mine and mine alone. Each one is marked with a nick on its ear. I have selected very carefully from among the sheep that Zophar was willing to sell. I trust no friend in such an endeavour. I check every mouth and every hoof. I feel very carefully every inch beneath the wool, in order to make sure of the state of health of each of the beasts in question. Zophar's prices were very generous. I have been haunting the sales for years, though until now, I have never been able to freely indulge my dream. I might have bested him on some of the prices. Someday my flock might well surpass his. His is a very competitive soul. Perhaps Zophar might someday regret the deal we have made.

Cursing the day when I was born.

Reaping the corn in the field.
Suckling at the breast.

"This is a boon for both of us, Job. I have more land than I can use for grazing at present. It is costing me nothing at all to share my meadow with you."

"You are generous in the extreme, Zophar. This way, I can build up my flock. It won't be long before I can afford to buy land of my own."

"We have made a perfect agreement. Your flocks will graze freely in my meadow. And in return, you will buy all of your sheep from me."

What is there to restrain the wicked?
Are not all things permitted under God?
If you had been wicked, would you be better off today?

I am the worst-possible Job! I am Job, the self-made man! A group of young shepherds stands before me! They ask an impossible boon! Their fathers are old and I have shed them from my employ! They are old, they are tired, they are worn out and of little use! The request is that I let these old fellows live and eat with my dogs! That they would patrol the edges of my flocks as the dogs now do! Why should I keep them on my dole? I have plenty of dogs to use! Since when is an old and worn-out man the equal of a good sheepdog? Let them go and live in the wilderness! Let them cut up mallow and feed on juniper roots! Let them dwell in cliffs or live in caves in the rocks! If I was old and worn and useless, I have no doubt that you would say the same to me!

A wadi is never the same. A highway for travelling caravans. A death-trap when it is flushed by sudden rains.

And God said, Let the Earth bring foorth grasse, the herbe yeelding seed, and the fruit tree, yeelding fruit after his kinde, whose seed is in it selfe, vpon the earth: and it was so.

I try not to sleep. If I find myself nodding, I shake myself awake. The last thing I want to do is to dream.

I am the worst-possible Job! I am Job, the self-made man! Standing beside a cliff! My men are struggling up the hillside! They are bringing up the body of one of my men! He has fallen while trying to rescue a kid which was trapped on the hillside! He slipped and landed on a ledge and broke his neck! It is sad to lose a good worker! I have known him from a boy! He has a wife and children! I will give my chief herdsman a few coins to give to the widow! I won't bother to visit the home! I don't care for gloomy wakes! The man is dead!

44

His luck has run out! There is nothing that I can do to bring him back! A serious loss! A good worker is always difficult to replace!

He shall save the humble person.
He shall deliver the island of the innocent.

We gain.

A mule and a human rode along.
If humans were mules said the man,
We mules would gladly carry twice the load.
If only God would hear and make this change.

Jemima, our first daughter. A girl with her father's temperament. I have always believed that she should have been a boy.

Many years ago now. A sunny morning, at sunrise. Watching the dust rise as the caravan trundles away.

Jemima stands beside her brother. Neither says a word, but I know what both are thinking. We have had this scene before. Jemima does not speak, but I know her thoughts. She has been stung by something that her brother has said in the past. We talked one day as her mother was washing clothing by the lagoon. I took a basketful of washing and began to walk towards the house and her mother began to soak the second basket of clothes as I walked away. I heard Jemima skip up beside me before I saw her. Father, why can I not go out, some day, on the caravans? We watched our uncles depart yesterday from the gates of the village, and as the camels began their trek, Mattan said that he would go out with the caravans some day. I said that I would go out too, and he turned to me and laughed. He said that he would go out with the caravans and fight the sandstorms and the brigands, and trade for silk and spices, while I would stay in our house in the village and spin wool and stir pottage and wash the clothes. Why, Father? Why? Why can Mattan go out on the caravans and I not go?

Not a word; no explanation - stroke him under the chin - cast away a perfect man - wickedness, recognized or unrecognized - praise him upon the loud cymbals - appreciate all that was said - a coin in my purse - to bring home to man his ignorance - pursue the dry stubble - the chaff which the wind driveth away.

"Perhaps your mother can explain it best. Perhaps you should talk to her, my daughter. Perhaps she can explain why things are as they are."

"No, Father! I have talked to her! I am asking you!"

"You ask me to explain why the sky is blue! You ask me to explain why the clouds are white! You ask me to explain why God made women and why God made men!"

A voice too dry to speak.
A land where everyone prospers.
Two men who share their secrets as they travel a road.

I am the worst-possible Job! I am Job, the self-made man! I have been asked to rescue an orphan! I refused to consider the plea! His father's body was found on the roadside! A band of brigands had made him their prey! Not a coin was left to the widow and her son! Why should people feel free to bring sad stories to me? The boy is far too young to employ. He would consume but not produce. It would set a precedent which I would be loathe to bear. Let every orphan fend for himself. My own father did little for me. All that I am, I have accomplished by myself. Better for him that he should make his way alone. Make my home an orphan's paradise, replete with coin and food and drink? Why should I be the one to rescue the dead man's son?

In God is my saluation, and my glorie: the rocke of my strength, and my refuge is in God.

Trust in him at all times; ye people, powre out your heart before him: God is a refuge for vs.

We lose.

Entering unto the springs of the sea.
Redeeming those in danger of death from famine.
Holding the soul of every living thing in my hand.

Sitting on the ash-heap. The five of us.

Camels, donkeys, trade and talk. A beggar feels in the dust for a coin. Lazy men tease busy girls at the well.

Bildad completes his speech of advice and takes a drink. I have barely been listening as he has been talking. Why did the silence only last for seven days? It was me who invited the talk. I am sorry now that I began this endless palaver. The three are well-meaning, I am sure. They offer words and words and words. Words of condolence and words that condemn. Words for the wise and words for the fool. They feel that they are near; I feel that they are far. They cannot possibly know what is bothering me.

No clouds gathered over the dry wadi.
It always seemed to happen without fail.
No rains fell, no flowers grew, nothing bloomed.
Many humans moved along the desert trail.

"I would make supplication to my judge. For he breaketh me with a tempest, and multiplieth my wounds without cause. He will not suffer me to take my breath, but filleth me with bitterness. Now my days are swifter than a post, they flee away, they see no good. They are passed away as the swift ships; as the eagle that hasteth to the prey. If I be wicked, why then labour I in vain? If I wash myself with snow water, and make my hands never so clean, yet shalt thou plunge me in the ditch, and mine own clothes shall abhor me. For he is not a man, as I am, that I should answer him, and we should come together in judgment. Let him take his rod away from me, and let not his fear terrify me. Then would I speak, and not fear him. I will say unto God, Do not condemn me. Shew me wherefore thou contendest with me. Hast thou eyes of flesh? Or seest thou as man seeth? Thou knowest that I am not wicked. Thou hast clothed me with skin and flesh, and hast fenced me with bones and sinews. Thou hast granted me life and favour. If I be wicked, woe unto me. And if I be righteous, yet will I not lift up my head. I am full of confusion. Therefore see thou mine affliction, for it increaseth. Thou huntest me as a fierce lion. Wherefore, then, hast thou brought me forth out of the womb? Oh that I had given up the ghost, and no eye had seen me! I should have been as though I had not been! I should have been carried from the womb to the grave! Are not my days few? Cease then, and let me alone, that I may take comfort a little!"

Stand in awe and sin not - reduced to an awed silence - live in the wilderness - perhaps he is there; perhaps he is not - man with a burdensome task - a mysterious storm, suddenly gathering and then clearing the air - ask me to explain - give ear to my words, o lord - unique in your relationship - insisted that I come.

I am the worst-possible Job! I am Job, the self-made man! A young shepherd at the village market! I have seen him buy and sell! He seems to know what qualities to look for in buying sheep! He has bested me once or twice! Some day he will be my rival! No doubt he wishes to expand his herd but lacks the means! I should take him into my employ! I should offer him one of my fields to graze his sheep! That way, I can cull the best lambs from his flock in the springtime, while he is toiling in my other fields, and give him my weakest ones! He will never catch on to my scheme! Let fools beware of fools-gold; it is only gold to a fool! I suspect that this game was played on me in my youth!

An old man talking to his son. Asking him to come closer. Asking which of his sons is he.

A young man giving a note to a trusted friend.
A boy speaking out in a gathering of elders.
Two travellers who make a solemn pact.

Listening to his voice. Feeling his arms. Giving his blessing.

God hath spoken once; twice haue I heard this, that power belongeth vnto God.
Also vnto thee, O Lord, belongeth mercie: for thou renderest to euery man according
to his worke.

May God give you dew from heaven. May God give you fertile fields. May God make many nations bow down to you.

I shared my dreams with Barachel on our two-day ride to his home. He seemed to understand my deepest concerns.

If only Barachel had been able to come to my side. He sent no word with his first-born son. He enjoined the young man to keep his silence.

What would Barachel say if he were here? His words I would no doubt be pleased to hear.

Does not prosperity increase with ungodliness?
Do you not cheat yourself if you do not cheat other men?
Why would God have made a world where this is so?

We endure.

I am the worst-possible Job! I am Job, the self-made man! I expect to grow old in my prosperity! My seed is established and my offspring gambol before my eyes! My house is safe from fear and neither is the rod of God upon me! My bulls engender and fail not and my cows calve and cast not their calves! My little ones are as a flock and my children dance! They take the timbrels and harp and rejoice at the sound of the organ! God has nothing to do with my prosperity! I am Job and I have built my house on my own! I expect to spend my days in wealth and go down in comfort to the grave!

Chapter 7

Five of us on the ash-heap. Zophar is our speaker.
A young man browsing in a market-place.
Zophar, the Shuhite. Has there ever been a Shuhite at a loss for words? Of course I cannot travel, but if I ever travel again, please, God, spare me from having to travel to the land of the Shuhites. My ears have been punished with years of their talk. There is nothing in what they say. Never a good word has ever come from out of that land. And Zophar is the worst. All he ever does is talk. When did I ever give him permission to call me a friend?

My skin is on fire. My life is in ashes. My children are dead.

The bulls of the wicked never fail. Their cows give birth and caste not their calves.

A family chanting around a glowing fire.
A terrible famine in a distant land.
A table groaning with benefice from the fields.

Their newborns grow like a flock and their children dance. They listen to the timbrel and the harp and rejoice at the sound of the organ.

Treading in the wine-press.
Taking my seat in the council of the elders.
Causing the widow's heart to sing.

They spend their days in wealth and go down with satisfaction to the grave.

What do other people say to you?
Do their words make any sense at all?
How could they be closer to God and his thoughts than are you?

Five of us on the ash-heap.
A young man buying sheep from his new-found friend.
Zophar. Zophar. Zophar. You assume that I wish to listen, but you are a fool. You would lecture a man who has fallen down a well. Your tongue is splendid, but your eyes are blind. Can't you see that your words are wasted? Your words are falling on the ears of a man in agony.

God teaches us more than the beasts.
He maketh us wiser than the fowles of heaven.

We hope.

Double to win. Double to win.
This is my motto. Double to win.
There are those who embrace life and those who give in.
This is my motto. Double to win.

Zophar is speaking, but I barely listen. Why would he want to talk to me? What could he possibly say to me that would make me feel better?

The air is fresh. The sky is blue. The clouds are white. On a day like this, I would have ridden my donkey out to my farthest field – the one with the trickling waterfall and the green grass in the meadow – and spent the day talking sheep with the shepherds who mind my flock.

It would have to be Zophar's turn to speak. He is eager, I can tell. The others have had their turn and Zophar has waited patiently, like an executioner slowly grinding away at his axe. Waiting for his moment in the proceedings. He looks around at the others. A pause to gather strength for his attack. He has no doubt that he speaks for God himself.

A dreadful sound is in his ears - the departure of my friends - a gesture of friendship - apparently, no answer is meant to be decisive - all they that see me - he tears my soul like a lion - endless palaver - the expectation of the poor - each plies a different route - the denial of the possibility of an answer.

"Oh that God would speak, and open his lips against thee, and that he would shew thee the secrets of wisdom. Know therefore that God exacteth of thee less than thine iniquity deserveth. Canst thou, by searching, find out God? Canst thou find out the Almighty? As high as heaven, what canst thou do? Deeper than hell, what canst thou know? He knoweth vain men. He seeth wickedness also. If thou prepare thine heart, and stretch out thine hands toward him; if iniquity be in thine hand, put it far away, and let not wickedness dwell in thy tabernacles, for then shalt thou lift up thy face without spot; yea, thou shalt be steadfast, and shalt not fear, because thou shalt forget thy misery, and remember it as waters that pass away. Thine age shall be clearer than the noonday. Thou shalt shine forth. Thou shalt be as the morning. And thou shalt be secure, because there is hope. Thou shalt lie down, and none shall make thee afraid. Yea, many shall make suit unto thee."

O Lord, rebuke me not in thy wrath: neither chasten me in thy hot displeasure.
For thine arrowes sticke fast in me; and thy hand presseth me sore.

Five of us on the ash-heap.
A pasture with lush grass and a sparkling spring.
Zophar is speaking. Zophar is droning on and on. Zophar, please leave off your speech-making for a brief moment and tell me what I need to know. Has the priest examined my garment? Has my plague changed its colour? Has my garment been burned in the fire? Has my plague spread or not? Am I unclean?

Touching the Almighty we cannot find him out.
He is excellent in power and in judgement and in justice.

We fear.

The tree neglected to eat and drink.
Its leaves and roots shrivelled and began to die.
The other trees in the forest wondered why.

Many years ago. When Eliphaz and I were both young men.
Almost ready to travel to the land of Tirzah. Almost ready to ask for the hand of the eldest daughter of Baruch.
All of my numbers are plump and pleasing. My donkeys, my camels, my horses. My fields, my crops, my yields. Eliphaz is passing through our village. He is leading a caravan. He is on his way to trade in the land of Tirzah. Eliphaz, my friend, I cannot travel today, I am afraid. I seem to be busy with many a problem. Raids on my folds by a band of brigands. A burst conduit which has flooded a field. A quarrel between one of my foremen and some of my men. A matter of whether the money they earned has been paid. I regret that I cannot accompany you. I will make up a caravan soon and travel that way. A gesture of friendship from Eliphaz. You say, Job, that you cannot come along and do your trading for yourself. Is there anything that I can help you with? Anything that I can sell at market on your behalf? Any message that you might wish to send to our old friend, Baruch? I think for a moment, and then I speak. Eliphaz, my friend, it so happens that I am anxious to settle a matter which has been a concern for quite some time. I beg leave to write a note. Please bear with me until I return. There is something, now that I think of it, that you can do for me when you visit the

land of Tirzah. All things ripen in their time. It is best to not leave things too late. I have a matter on my mind whose time, I believe, has come.

Binding floods from overflowing.
Clothing myself with righteousness.
Overturning men in the night so they are destroyed.

"Please be sure to give this note to Baruch. Deliver it promptly, as soon as you arrive. This letter, my friend, is very important to me."

"A sealed note? Keeping secrets? Does Job no longer trust his closest friend?"

"A private matter. Hardly a secret. I promise you that you shall know all about it soon enough."

Has anyone suffered as you have suffered?
Has anyone known an equal ordeal?
What could give them any sense of the depth of your loss?

Five of us on the ash-heap.
A herd of sheep grazing silently on a hillside.
Zophar is speaking, but my mind wanders back to the past. Has he forgotten what has passed between us? What would make him so bold as to call me a friend? What is the meaning of friendship? If I were dangling from a cliff, would Zophar pause in his journey to market and spend even one of his precious moments to save my life? Would he pause in the business of the building up of his herds and flocks and stop along the trail and rescue me?

The mountains are always there. There for the shepherd. There for the sheep. The lush valleys, the verdant meadows, the fragrant hills.

And God said, Let there bee lights in the firmament of the heauen, to diuide the day from the night: and let them be for signes and for seasons, and for dayes and yeeres.

Surely it is my wife. Of course. It has to be. Why did the obvious thought not occur to me until now?

The little boy who brings the food and drink. He must be a grandchild of one of her friends. Sent, each day, to the ash-heap, by my wife.

I must remember to thank my wife for her thoughtfulness.

Five of us on the ash-heap.
A young man with a pen of sickly lambs.

The great Zophar is speaking, but my mind is constantly wandering. Have I answered him as yet? What did I say to him? Did I put him in his place? Why would I waste my time in talking to one who never listens? Many times I have tried to talk sense to Zophar, but he is always the one with plenty to say. If I speak, he doesn't listen. He merely pauses in his speech and waits impatiently for me to say a word or two. Then he continues on with his endless palaver.

Mortal man is not more just than God.
Man is not more pure than his maker.

We rejoice.

You say that you want to talk, my daughter.
Though silence was golden before.
It is words that leave the deepest wounds.
I would rather you use a knife.

Heber, our second son, has a dilemma.

He is brooding silently as the days go by. He is faced with choice and cannot decide, so he broods and broods.

There is the girl at the well – a shy smile and a dress with colourful patches – whose father has nothing to offer. Nothing, that is, but good will, a kind heart and a charming daughter. And what about the widow? She whose husband has left her six fields, four of them most desirable. Sunlit hillsides, sparking rivulets, grazing sheep. A most challenging dilemma. Day after day, he broods alone in silence. His brothers and his sisters have told us of his agony. He has said not a word on the topic to us, his parents. Heber sits at the table and broods. He sits by the fire and daydreams. He closes the sheep-gate and stares off into the distance. Perhaps today he will speak of his thoughts. Perhaps tomorrow he will make an announcement. Will it be a splendid wedding? The fatted calf? The flowing wine? The dance of celebration at the widow's fine house? Or will it be a modest ceremony? An apologetic father? A subdued but happy mother of a blushing bride? Time will tell. Plenty of time to brood and ponder, ponder and brood. His brothers and sisters say that he has never asked their advice. No doubt he wants no advice from his parents. He only wants time to brood and ponder, ponder and brood. In the meantime, we sit at the table breaking bread and sipping wine, discussing the small talk of the day and the topics of the seasons, while Heber sits and pokes at his food.

What looks like a child - sipping cold water and hatching a plan - nothing to offer -
the earth shook and trembled - containing elements of truth - make a fire at night - plagued

with other things - seems no answer at all - a man whom god correcteth - there was none to save them.

"Today we will go to the southern-most field. There is much there to do."

"Yes, Father."

"The thicket fencing needs shoring up. It is showing its age. It is never good to put things off for too long."

Scar-tissue gleaming in the glow of a fire.
A load of grain rotting on a granary floor.
A barefoot girl dancing at a wedding.

Five of us on the ash-heap.
A young man arguing fiercely with another young man.
Zophar is speaking. I am finding it very hard to concentrate on what he is saying. My mind keeps wandering away from the business at hand. I can only think of Barachel, my oldest friend. Barachel is ailing. He has sent his first-born son. He would have come, himself, if he were able. I am forced to listen to Zophar, but I would rather think of Barachel, my friend.

My wounds stinke, and are corrupt: because of my foolishnesse.
I am troubled, I am bowed downe greatly; I goe mourning all the day long.

We mourn.

Multiplying my days.
Giving counsel unto others.
Covering myself with dust and ashes.

A wonderful day. A wonderful day. A wonderful day.

I would love to be out in my meadow. Filling my flask at the trickling stream. Watching my sheep quietly grazing in the grass.

I have barely listened to Zophar as he has spoken. My mind has been plagued with other things. His speech was not for me. It was not a speech of comfort, nor an attempt to help a friend. It was an opportunity to impress the other speakers and put himself in the right with God above. Come down from your perch on a cloud, Zophar. Zophar, the wise! Zophar, the all-knowing! Zophar, the confidant of God! Comeuppance is an axe which cuts both ways. It is time he was put in his place. I will look him in the eye and speak my mind.

A young shepherd was menaced by two fierce wolves.

He remembered the advice of his wise friend.
The young shepherd reached out and stroked the two fierce wolves underneath their chins.

The two wolves became placid. Almost friends.

"I am as one mocked of his neighbour, who calleth upon God, and he answereth him. The just upright man is laughed to scorn. Lo, mine eye hath seen all this, mine ear hath heard and understood it. What ye know, the same do I know also. I am not inferior unto you. Surely I would speak to the Almighty, and I desire to reason with God. Hear now my reasoning, and hearken to the pleadings of my lips. Behold now, I have ordered my cause; I know that I shall be justified. Call thou, and I will answer: or let me speak, and answer thou me. How many are mine iniquities and sins? Make me to know my transgression and my sin. Wherefore hidest thou thy face, and holdest me for thine enemy? Wilt thou break a leaf driven to and fro? And wilt thou pursue the dry stubble? Man that is born of a woman is of few days, and full of trouble. He cometh forth like a flower, and is cut down: he fleeth also as a shadow, and continueth not. Seeing his days are determined, the number of his months are with thee, thou hast appointed his bounds that he cannot pass. Man dieth, and wasteth away: yea, man giveth up the ghost, and where is he? As the waters fail from the sea, and the flood decayeth and drieth up, so man lieth down, and riseth not. Till the heavens be no more, they shall not awake, nor be raised out of their sleep. The mountain falling cometh to nought, and the rock is removed out of his place. The waters wear the stones, thou washest away the things which grow out of the dust of the earth, and thou destroyest the hope of man. Thou prevailest for ever against him, and he passeth. Thou changest his countenance, and sendest him away. His sons come to honour, and he knoweth it not; and they are brought low, but he perceiveth it not of them. His flesh upon him shall have pain, and his soul within him shall mourn."

A son who is precious - teach us to number our days - I am forced to listen - he that *took me out of the womb - the possibility of an answer - recognize me and take me in - the* *loss of our children - almost friends - dogs have compassed me - my father and mother* *forsake me.*

Five of us on the ash-heap.
A young man with lambs which he cannot sell.
Zophar is still speaking. Why does he persist? His words are most unwelcome in my ears. Here is a man who thinks only of himself. A man for whom other people are stepping stones on his way across a stream that lies in his path. A man who rides upon one's back when the way is steep and narrow and then, when it is his turn to lend his back to the enterprise, in a fair and pleasant meadow, declines to take his turn as he is too tired.

A man with his people in bondage. A man with a burdensome task. A man who is charged with doing the work of a god.

A man whose wife brings food and water.
A young boy taking his place in a circle of men.
A lion's cough growing louder and louder.

No light for days and days. A god in all his anger. A god whose word is law.

Forsake me not, O Lord: O my God, be not farre from me.
Make haste to helpe mee, O Lord my saluation.

A plague of locusts. The deaths of sons. Surely this must be the darkest day.

Wending my way on a mountain pass. Riding along a trail, many years ago, in the land of the Buzites.

I hear a call for help. A man is trapped on a ledge with a broken ankle. I climb down and offer assistance. He clings to my back on the side of the mountain. Sheer rock and a gorge below. We might soon be a heap of bones on the canyon floor.

The man is Barachel, the Buzite, of the kindred of the Ram. "A friend for life", he solemnly pledges, as he rides along on my donkey. "I owe a great debt to you, my friend. My life is in your hands. Call on me at any time and I will come to your aid."

Are you unique as a sufferer?
Is your wife unique in her loss?
Are you unique in your relationship with God?

We pray.

Five of us on the ash-heap. Zophar is giving a speech.
A young man alone in a field with a tattered dream.
Zophar, stop talking and help me. My flesh is burning me alive. My skin is so hot that I cry aloud. My eyes are cloudy. I cannot see. Is there a bright white spot on my skin? Is it reddish or is it white? Has leprosy broken out? Am I unclean?

Chapter 8

I am staggering through the underbrush! Being hunted like a wild boar! Hearing the yelps of the scavenging hyena-men! Thorns tear at my clothing and rip at my flesh! My hair is dirty and matted! I am terrified that they will catch me! I will be torn from limb to limb! I stagger from exhaustion! How long have I been running? I fling myself down and pant in a bed of leaves!

Where is wisdom to be found? Where is the place of understanding?

Two young men sipping cold water and hatching a plan.
A daughter who struggles with a bucket at a well.
A man amazed at his success in winning a bride.

It is hid from the eyes of the living, and kept secret from the fowls of the air.

Seeing the ways of men and all his goings.
Hearing the painful cry of the afflicted.
Knowing the path to the house where light dwells.

Destruction and death have listened closely. Rumours of wisdom have reached their ears.

How have you treated other people?
Has kindness been your watchword?
Have you not cast certain men from out of your midst?

I lie panting in a bed of leaves! I hear foot-steps coming near! I am hunted by the hyena-men! They hold me in derision! They long to spit in my face! I have disdained to set their fathers with the dogs of my flock! They live solitary in want and famine! They cut up mallows by the bushes and juniper roots for their meat! They have been driven from among us as we drive out thieves from our midst! I hear footsteps in the leaves! I jump up and start to run! I can hear them running behind me! They are chasing me through the scrub-land! I hear snarling and panting and whimpering! They will destroy me if they catch me! They are vile! They are cruel! They hunt in packs!

Decree a thing and it shall be established unto thee.
A light shall shine upon thy ways.

We laugh.

The sun and the pole star in the distance.
Each plies a different route across the sky.
Each looks at the other; neither blinks.
Am I the master here or are you?

Eliphaz is speaking. This is his second speech. Surely he said enough the first time. Do asininities turn to wisdom with repetition?

The eyes of Eliphaz bore into mine. As relentless as a lion when it stalks its prey. I can barely hear the words that he is saying.

Eliphaz has been waiting for this opportunity for years. For a chance to place himself squarely on the side of God. To bring the word of God and Eliphaz to the lowly Job.

As chaff before the wind - graven with an iron pen - raises as many new questions as it answers - stagger from exhaustion - joy cometh in the morning - he flattereth himself in his own eyes - a light shall shine - the writhing of the tortured thought - milk left out in the sun - it will become placid.

"The wicked man travaileth with pain all his days, and the number of years is hidden to the oppressor. A dreadful sound is in his ears: in prosperity the destroyer shall come upon him. He believeth not that he shall return out of darkness, and he is waited for of the sword. He wandereth abroad for bread, saying, Where is it? He knoweth that the day of darkness is ready at his hand. Trouble and anguish shall make him afraid; they shall prevail against him, as a king ready to the battle. For he stretcheth out his hand against God, and strengtheneth himself against the Almighty. He runneth upon him, even on his neck, upon the thick bosses of his bucklers: because he covereth his face with his fatness, and maketh collops of fat on his flanks. And he dwelleth in desolate cities, and in houses which no man inhabiteth, which are ready to become heaps. He shall not be rich, neither shall his substance continue, neither shall he prolong the perfection thereof upon the earth. He shall not depart out of darkness; the flame shall dry up his branches, and by the breath of his mouth shall he go away. Let not him that is deceived trust in vanity: for vanity shall be his recompence. It shall be accomplished before his time, and his branch shall not be green. He shall shake off his unripe grape as the vine, and shall cast off his flower as the olive. For the congregation of hypocrites shall be desolate, and fire shall consume the tabernacles of bribery. They conceive mischief, and bring forth vanity, and their belly prepareth deceit."

God be mercifull vnto vs, and blesse vs: and cause his face to shine vpon vs.
That thy way may bee knowen vpon earth, thy sauing health among all nations.

Stumbling into a ditch! The burs snatch at my clothing! The briars cling to my hair! I spin around as I hear something moving! What is this? What is this? Can this be a human being? No human eyes should contain that much fear! It is a creature of some kind, that is for sure! It is dressed in rags and has streaks of mud on its cheeks and its hair is dishevelled! It is difficult to believe that it is a woman, with such fear in her eyes! But why is she all alone here? What a terrible place to be left lying down all alone! She must be ill or she would crawl away from this place! I move towards her as she cowers in fear! What is it that she is hiding? Is she not alone?

Happy is a man whom God correcteth.
Despise not thou the chastening of the Almighty.

We cry.

A man was alone on the desert.
He cursed his vile luck.
I am a hyena, he said to himself.
There are no people here for me to scavenge.

Bildad and I as partners. Many years ago.
Waiting for his return on the edge of town.
Bildad is riding on a donkey. Our drivers are walking behind in a broken line. The villagers are gathered at the gates to watch them arrive. Bildad and the drivers take forever to reach the village. All of them covered in dust. All of them quiet and broken. I run ahead to meet him. Bildad, what has happened? Did you not keep enough mules for your men? Does money mean that much to you that you would begrudge these men a ride? Surely the price for the grain was double. Surely you are carrying a fortune in your travel-bag. His face is dirty and his lip has been split. His eyes are whirling furiously. Something is terribly wrong. Job, a terrible thing has happened! I don't know how to tell you! A disaster which could not be controlled! There was a howling angry mob! They threatened my life and took the money! There was nothing that I could do! You would have had to do the same! Everyone there was

out for my blood! They had clubs and pitchforks and spears! They claimed that I had cheated them! They refused to let me leave town! They took almost every cent that we had gained!

Chanting psalms around the fire.
Thinking of questions that I would like to ask of God.
Listening to friends who give advice.

"Did you sell the gain and the donkeys? Where is the money? Let me see! Is it true that grain was selling at twice the price?"

"Yes I sold the grain! I sold the donkeys as well! After the sale, I held a fortune in my hands!

"Well tell me what has happened! Why do you hold out so few coins! How could so much grain yield so little at twice the price?"

How have you been treated by other people?
Has kindness been their watch-word in dealing with you?
Have other people not cast you out of their midst?

I am afraid to stay here and look! I am stunned! Who would have thought? This dishevelled bundle of rags is a human mother! A human mother suckling what looks like a child! The woman's eyes are terrified! She is terrified of me! She draws the rags up close to her, trying to cover her baby's face! I stand in the ditch and stare at her! Brackish water up to my knees! I duck down and look around and sniff the air! What if her hyena-husband should return with some of his pack? The nursing mother is terrified! The baby sucks desperately at the teat! I turn away and scramble up the side of the ditch!

The desert sands are always shifting. At times a howling, raging menace. A graveyard for travellers lost in a storm.

And God said, Let the waters bring foorth aboundantly the mouing creature that hath life, and foule that may flie aboue the earth in the open firmament of heauen.

When I find myself drifting off into dreams, I jerk awake in an agonized sweat.

Stuffing roots into my mouth! Not knowing what they are, but needing sustenance, or I will faint along the way! Drinking brackish water! Lying down in a hole I scoop out of the ground! Dragging leaves and branches over me! Protection from eyes and claws! I lie in the darkness, listening for sounds! A lion's cough! A hyena's chuckle! A number of frightening sounds! I lie still and barely breathe! I try not to make any noise! I listen very carefully! Could some of them be sneaking up to attack me?

God bindeth the flood from overflowing.
The thing that is hid he bringeth forth to light.

We wonder.

A cobbler is berated in the marketplace.
Princes, kings and potentates speak in anger.
Torn threads, sagging leather, uneven soles.
They all demand that the cobbler make repairs.

The winds are howling and the sands bite deep.

I am muffled up like a mummy. Epher, our second son, plods behind me. A string of camels, tied together, one by one, moves through the storm.

We paused, when the storm arose, and our leader considered. I believe we should push on ahead. Tie all of the camels together. Just follow along, one by one, and we will be fine. I turn to Epher, our third son, who has waited outside the circle of the men. Will you be all right on your own? Yes, Father. I'm sure I will. We plod along on our camels, each in his own separate world. Robes wrapped around our bodies, hoods and scarves pulled tight around our heads. Each thinking his own thoughts, of the days past and of the future. Nothing can be thought of the present of the storm. It is simply a case of waiting as the camel moves along, one foot in front of the other. Time is measured by one more footprint in the sand. The howling wind and the grit between the teeth. The eyes protected by a hood from the welter of the storm. What would there be to see if one peeked through the folds? Nothing but sand and sand and sand and sand and sand. How does the old fellow know where we are going? How can he track these wastes in the face of this blinding sand? How is Epher doing behind me? Is he regretting his decision to ride on his own? Regrets for the times when Father would hoist him up by his side? Plenty of time to do one's thinking in the midst of a sandstorm. He has heard stories around the campfires. Does he think that this is one of the worst or one of the least? Well, this is his sandstorm at any rate. The one he has braved all alone without the help of his father. The one that he might look back on some day as a milestone of sorts. And now, the winds have quieted down. We stop and make an assessment. We shake our robes free from sand and take our drinks. Epher comes and joins the assessment circle. He takes his place among the men of the caravan. No one looks askance. Least of all me.

The power of thine anger - the question is never lost sight of - assininities turn to wisdom - labour and sorrow - wandereth abroad for bread - in the evening is cut down - twisting in the chains of his logic - roots shall be dried up - cut down like the grass - restoreth my soul.

"Quite the storm. A very strong wind. A curtain of sand."

"And what of our course? Have we held to the track?"

"As true as can be. We were right to push on. We saved half a day's ride."

A whirlwind spinning like a child's top.
Grain which sells at twice the price.
The arrival of a group of friends.

I stagger along towards the village! It has to be somewhere ahead! I must find my home and my friends! I must return to the bosom of my family! There was a time when I was a wrestler! The greatest wrestler of my tribe! I could have broken the backs of the best of them over my knee! I do not belong out here! I am not a human jackal! I have my faults, but I should not have to live like these people do! What have I descended to? My leg is hurting badly! My limp is quite pronounced! My clothes are torn and ragged! My hair is quite dishevelled! Perhaps that is what will help me! Perhaps it will let me pass for one of them!

Let the people praise thee, O God; let all the people praise thee.
O let the nations be glad, and sing for ioy: for thou shalt iudge the people righteously; and gouerne the nations vpon earth.

We doubt.

Plucking the spoil out of the teeth of the wicked.
Binding the unicorn in the furrow.
Setting up high those that be low.

Eliphas comes to the end of his second speech. He sits back on the ash-heap and waits for me to reply. He looks around at the others. Is he expecting to hear applause? He licks his lips like a lion who has swallowed his prey.

I have barely heard what he has been saying. My mind has been busy with other things.

What is the use of making reply to Eliphaz or any of the others? Such as Eliphaz will never be convinced by what I say. He has not come here to listen, but to pontificate. Eliphas sits on an ash-heap, but he speaks from a mountain-top. My contention is not with Eliphaz, but with God.

An elder brother spoke in jest to his younger brother.
My inheritance to you for a mess of pottage.
I will put my word in writing – in the water.

"My breath is corrupt, my days are extinct, the graves are ready for me. Are there not mockers with me? And doth not mine eye continue in their provocation? Lay down now, put me in a surety with thee; who is he that will strike hands with me? For thou hast hid their heart from understanding: therefore shalt thou not exalt them. He that speaketh flattery to his friends, even the eyes of his children shall fail. He hath made me also a byword of the people; and aforetime I was as a tabret. Mine eye also is dim by reason of sorrow, and all my members are as a shadow. Upright men shall be astonied at this, and the innocent shall stir up himself against the hypocrite. The righteous also shall hold on his way, and he that hath clean hands shall be stronger and stronger. But as for you all, do ye return, and come now: for I cannot find one wise man among you. My days are past, my purposes are broken off, even the thoughts of my heart. They change the night into day: the light is short because of darkness. If I wait, the grave is mine house: I have made my bed in the darkness. I have said to corruption, Thou art my father: to the worm, Thou are my mother, and my sister. And where is now my hope? As for my hope, who shall see it? They shall go down to the bars of the pit, when our rest together is in the dust."

Thoughts of more important things - the light of thy countenance - left lying down all alone - recall our attention to the original question - thy law is within my heart - I shall not want - protection from eyes and claws - I am feeble and sore broken - judge through the curtain of the clouds - passed away in a wrath.

Do these people live in families? Are they human after all? Would that woman be waiting for her loved-one? Would he be pleased to see her again? Would he have been scavenging for their welfare? Would he have been worried about his child? Perhaps I should go back there! Perhaps I should go back to that woman who was suckling her child and talk to her! I believe I am close to the village! It is a long way back I am sure! The others would never accept me! They would tear me limb from limb! And if she should still be lying there and feeding her little child, why then what would I say?

A man with a son. A son who is precious. A man with a son to whom he has never, ever lied.

Stories of dry wells and arid streams.
A letter which is entrusted to a friend.
A young boy with an arm-load of kindling.

I see the wood, I see the coals, I see the knife. The son is asking questions. The son is curious about the coming sacrifice.

Let the people praise thee, O God, let all the people praise thee.

Then shall the earth yeeld her increase; and God, euen our owne God, shall blesse vs.

The father whispers softly. The lord will provide. The lord will provide. The lord will provide.

What would Barachel have said had he been here?

How low have you been humbled?
To what levels have you lowered other men?
Are there depths from which no man can ever return?

We affirm.

I am old and I am tired! I want only to go home! I hope that this is the trail to the village! Surely someone will recognize me and take me in! A warm bath, some food and drink and some decent clothing, and I will no doubt look like Job once again! What is that growling noise I hear? There must be someone ahead on the trail! It is a snarling pack of hyena-men! There are more of them this time! They pause and sniff the air! They whimper and snarl and break into a jog-trot! They are rabid and their fangs are bared! They are approaching me and snarling like a pack of wolves!

Chapter 9

Five of us on the ash-heap. Bildad's second speech.
Two young men sipping cold water and hatching a plan.
Bildad reaches for the jug. He raises it to his lips and wets his throat. He waits for my nod so he can speak. How long has he been thinking of what he is going to say? Did he practice his speech on the way here from the land of the Shuhites? Did he measure his phrases as he rode along the trail? Or did he think of these things to say the moment he heard of my misfortune? He sets the jug aside. I nod, and Bildad begins to speak.

My skin is on fire. My life is in ashes. My children are dead.

God is high in the height of his heaven. How high are the highest stars?

Looking for a boy in a crowd of children.
A man who yearns to hear what his friend would say.
Two shepherds peering over the edge of a cliff.

How can God see what we see here on the ground? How can he judge through the curtain of the clouds?

Riding my donkey along a trail.
Rejoicing as my children grow and learn.
Exchanging opinions with my friends.

Thick clouds obscure his sight. He cannot see us as he walks the circuit of heaven.

Do you know what has happened before you?
Were your ancestors free from cares?
How did they react when such things happened to them?

Five of us on the ash-heap. Bildad's second speech.
A caravan of mules with bulging sacks of grain.
Does he have a standard speech for all to hear? He sits on the ash-heap and mourns my children, but they were not his. He will go home, when this mourning period is over, and clutch his children and his grandchildren to his breast.

God is mighty and despiseth not any.
He is mighty in strength and wisdom.

We flourish.

A man sinks low until his knees touch the sand.
The circles of the bird draw small and tight.
The dry wind blisters the man and preens the bird.

Bildad is speaking. Why must he torture me with words? Bildad gives speeches in which he says that there have been too many speeches.
I let his words wash over me while I struggle with thoughts of more important things.
This is his second speech. How many speeches do these friends of mine intend to make? Was not everything said in the first few words after Bildad opened his mouth?

Away as with a flood - there is a purpose in it all - close my ears - god is our refuge and our strength - in fear of every footstep - the presence of mine enemies - send out thy light and thy truth - a gate in a narrow lane - to be understood in good time - teach god knowledge.

"Yea, the light of the wicked shall be put out, and the spark of his fire shall not shine. The light shall be dark in his tabernacle, and his candle shall be put out with him. The steps of his strength shall be straitened, and his own counsel shall cast him down. For he is cast into a net by his own feet, and he walketh upon a snare. The gin shall take him by the heel, and the robber shall prevail against him. The snare is laid for him in the ground, and a trap for him in the way. Terrors shall make him afraid on every side, and shall drive him to his feet. His strength shall be hunger-bitten, and destruction shall be ready at his side. It shall devour the strength of his skin: even the firstborn of death shall devour his strength. His confidence shall be rooted out of his tabernacle, and it shall bring him to the king of terrors. It shall dwell in his tabernacle, because it is none of his: brimstone shall be scattered upon his habitation. His roots shall be dried up beneath, and above shall his branch be cut off. His remembrance shall perish from the earth, and he shall have no name in the street. He shall be driven from light into darkness, and chased out of the world. He shall neither have son nor nephew among his people, nor any remaining in his dwellings. They that come after him shall be astonied at his day, as they that went before were affrighted. Surely such are the dwellings of the wicked, and this is the place of him that knoweth not God."

How amiable are thy tabernacles, O Lord of hostes!
My soule longeth, yea euen fainteth for the courts of the Lord: my heart and my flesh cryeth out for the liuing God.

Five of us on the ash-heap. Bildad's second speech.
Frenzied bidding in a famished town.
Why would I want to listen to him? I cannot keep my mind from wandering. Why should I even try? Friendship is that which curdles, like milk left out in the sun. It is that which fades away. It is that which turns on one's heel and stings one as one walks along life's path.

God withdraweth not his eyes from the righteous.
He doth establish them forever and they are exalted.

We falter.

A hyena looked a lion in the eye.
I contribute more than you to life on the earth.
When I have time I am going to make a list.

Zophar and I. When we were young and sharing our dreams.
My spring trip to the land of the Naahamites. My first trip to see my lambs. Wonderful thoughts of the trickling rivulets and the waving grasses of the meadow and the mountain breeze.
Walking across the meadow. Zophar with a worried look on his brow. He greets me and then he takes me to show me the pens. His men are gathered around and leaning on the thickets which hold the sheep. I open the gate and examine my first brood of lambs. I cannot believe what I am seeing. This is the poorest brood of lambs that I have ever seen. I have haunted the markets of the sheep-sellers. The land of Uz, the land of the Temanites, the land of the Shuthiutes, the land of the Nammanites. Zophar's sheep are not the only sheep that I have seen. I have studied the shepherd's lore and I know what I know. Puny, sickly, feeble. I move from lamb to lamb. Are there no healthy ones among them? What has happened to my flock? I check the ears. Already marked. I have no workers in the field. The birthing and the nicking of the ears has all been done by Zophar's men. Zophar opens my gate as I brush on past him. I hurry to his pen and push open the gate and I kneel. Healthy, healthy, healthy. Every one a healthy lamb. What kind of agreement have I made with what kind of man? I rise to my feet and face the partner of my dreams.

Looking to the ends of the earth.
Knowing the ordinances of heaven.
Giving light to him that is in misery.

"I agree with what you say, Job, but I have no explanation. You yourself examined each sheep as we made the sale. There was nothing wrong with any of the sheep which you bought."

"My lambs are smaller, feebler, punyer. Your lambs are healthy and full of life. I was not able to be here when the lambs were born."

"I have no idea what has happened, Job. My men are as honest as the day is long. Those lambs are your lambs for certain, I have no doubt."

Do you think of ancient stories as you go about your day?
Are the ancient stories the stuff of your deepest dreams?
What does the voice of these ancient stories have to say?

Five of us on the ash-heap. Bildad's second speech.
A young man sleeping on bags of golden coins.
Bildad is speaking. Oh why does he torture me? Let Bildad vent his wisdom on some other friend who has suffered great loss. Let him go to another land and make his speech. Oh, how I wish that my ears had lids as my eyes have. I would close my ears and not hear a word that he says.

A wadi is never the same. Bone dry when one is thirsty. At other times, cool shade amid leafy trees.

And God created great whales, and euery liuing creature that moueth, which the
waters brought forth aboundantly after their kinde, and euery winged foule after his kinde:
and God saw that it was good.

My wife brings food and water.
"The little boy has just been here. Only a few minutes ago."
That look of irritation. "What little boy do you mean?"
"Was it not you who sent the boy?"
"What boy? What message did he bring? Food? Not food from me! Can't you see I have brought you food – here in this bowl? Your lack of sustenance has made you light-headed. Leave off the babbling and eat your food and drink your drink. What is all this nonsense about a little boy?"

Five of us on the ash-heap. Bildad's second speech.
An angry mob complaining of tainted grain.
Bildad speaks as if his words are a balm for my skin, but still I suffer. There is a plague upon my head. There is a plague upon my beard. It is deeper than the skin. My hair is yellow and thin. It is dry scall, as anyone can see. It is leprosy, I am sure. I am unclean.

God is mighty and despiseth not any.
He is mighty in strength and wisdom.

We gain.

A mule and a human rode along.
If mules were human said the mule,
We would generously give our mules twice the feed.
If only God would hear and make this change.

Bazak, our fourth son, is working on a problem.
Each time a caravan comes through from the south, he talks to the merchants and the camel-drivers.
He has heard that there is a land of plenty. A land of silks and satins and pearls. A land where the river overflows in the springtime and the crops are always abundant year after year. The seasons are relied on there – none of the droughts that we have to deal with and none of the floods that plague our land with incessant rains. There the trade-routes cross from the ends of the earth and everyone is welcome. Whatever religion, whatever tribe, whatever tongue. There a man can build up his holdings. Buy a fine home and spectacular rings. Return to his homeland in regal splendour. Buy up fields and houses and heaping stores of grains. Do you think I should go, Father? One of these days? They say it's a land where everyone prospers. I don't mind living in my father's house. That is certainly as it should be. But what of the future? What will I think then? I would be living on the charity of the first-born of my brothers. I would never feel that anything was mine. There, a man is a man in his own right. There, he succeeds with a wave of his hand. There, the merchants live like princes and the landowners live like kings. I am not getting any younger, Father. I should really decide quite soon. All of this from our fourth son, Bazak, as we mend a gate in a narrow lane. I hold the gate against the post as he drives a nail with a rock. The gate is to keep the dogs from running away.

Menaced by a fierce wolf - like grass which groweth up - the food, the wine and the talk - the workers of iniquity - with the practical issue in mind - you needed water; you needed food - to make the desert bloom - oh that I had wings like a dove - many more stories to tell - the penal result of sin.

"Do you think that Mother would be heartbroken if I were to leave?"

"Your mother would be very sad, but she would adjust."

"I would miss the gatherings at the houses. All of the family there together. The food, the wine and the talk."

A man who wishes that his friend had not arrived.
A young lamb lying bleating on a ledge.
A boy who yearns for authority with the men.

Five of us on the ash-heap. Bildad's second speech.
A young man showing his friend his empty hands.

There was a day when life was simpler. A blue sky, white clouds, the warm of the sunshine. Water trickling down from the mountains, a meadow of grazing ewes, a drink of soothing water from a stream.

Yea the sparrowe hath found an house, and the swallow a nest for her selfe, where
she may lay her young, euen thine altars, O Lord of hostes, my king and my God.
Blessed are they that dwell in thy house: they wilbe still praysing thee.

We lose.

Resting in the coolness of the shade.
Wondering that the hawk knows how to fly.
Eating bread with my siblings at my house.

Bildad finishes his speech.

I thought that he would never come to an end. Bildad is never so generous as when his gift is confined to words.

Should I tell him that I have barely been listening? Should I tell him that I have not been soothed by his words? So shallow is his wisdom that there are children who could say what he has said.

We clouds should all have a meeting.
Every cloud on the earth in one big room.
We clouds need to draw up a schedule.
It will tell us when to make the desert bloom.

"God hath also kindled his wrath against me, and he counteth me unto him as one of his enemies. His troops come together, and raise up their way against me, and encamp round about my tabernacle. He hath put my brethren far from me, and mine acquaintance are verily estranged from me. My kinsfolk have failed, and my familiar friends have forgotten me. Yea, young children despised me; I arose, and they spake against me. All my inward friends abhorred me: and they whom I loved are turned against me. My bone cleaveth to my skin and to my flesh, and I am escaped with the skin of my teeth. Have pity upon me, have pity upon me, O ye my friends; for the hand of God hath touched me. Why do ye persecute me as God, and are not satisfied with my flesh? Oh that my words were now written! Oh that they were printed in a book! That they were graven with an iron pen and lead in the rock for ever! For I know that my redeemer liveth, and that he shall stand at the latter day upon the earth. And though after my skin worms destroy this body, yet in my flesh shall I see God."

Noticed these weighty cares - give us help from trouble - the sparrowe hath found an house - the raising of practical difficulties - forming myself out of clay - an house which he builded not - the question that puzzles - graven with an iron pen - a man stands on a mountain top - a dry and thirsty land where no water is.

Five of us on the ash-heap. Bildad's second speech.
A young man questioning members of the caravans.
Oh Bildad, please desist! My agony will not be soothed by endless speeches. My complaint will not be answered with human words. It is God with whom I wish to speak. You have no authority to speak on behalf of God.

An old man near the end of his days. An old man with his life fulfilled. An old man who blesses his first-born son.

Two men on a two-day trek with one mule.
Shepherds marking lambs with a nick in the ear.
A dance of celebration at a fine house.

I give him fertile fields. I give him grain and wine. I call on my god to give him dew from heaven.

Blessed is the man whose strength is in thee: in whose heart are the wayes of them:
Who passing through the valley of Baca, make it a well: the raine also filleth the pooles.

I have followed God's ways and he has blessed me. I have walked in the paths of righteousness. I have heeded the word of God in all his commands.

Walking along with my donkey. Barachel riding on his back. He insists that we take turns, but he is injured and I insist that only he should ride.

Another rider joins us. A rough-looking fellow. Knife in his belt; scars on his face. Barachel tells the story of Job and the rescue. The rider turns to Barachel and says, "So he is sacred, is he?" and rides away.

"What was that all about?" I ask.

"He is a local brigand, Job. He was after the money in your purse – at the expense, perhaps, of your life – but I waved him away. Today, my friend, we have saved each other's life!"

What is the meaning of all these old stories?
What is the meaning of what happens to you?
Could there be any connection between the two?

We endure.

Five of us on the ash-heap. Bildad's second speech.
A young man with a dream in tatters and a prosperous friend.
Is Bildad still speaking? I thought I had answered him. But what is the use, as he will simply make a third speech in which he repeats what he has said again and again. The sun is hot. The air is dry. My throat is parched. Where is the flask? It is usually here. Has the young boy brought cold water from the well?

Chapter 10

My sons and daughters are at their feast! I see them talking and laughing! They are seated in a circle! Mattan, our first-born son; Jemima, our first daughter; Heber, our second son; Epher, our third son; Bazak, our fourth son; Kezia, our second daughter; Evron, our fifth son; Avram, our sixth son; Noach, our seventh son; and Karen, our youngest daughter! They are in the courtyard of a house! It is Mattan's house! Our eldest, Mattan, is speaking! Our first-born son! Let me tell you of the time when I dumped a load of Father's grain on the granary floor ... The sun is shining! The sky is clear! A perfect day! Our children's children sit on the ground and on their parents' knees! Our children chuckle at the stories as they sip their wine!

I want to speak with the Almighty. I desire to reason with God.

Two men meeting a young girl at a well.
A brood of lambs enclosed inside a thicket.
A caravan of mules with bulging sacks.

I take my flesh in my teeth. I grasp my life in my hand.

Making a hedge about my favourites.
Saving the poor from the sword.
Striking wicked men in the open sight of others.

Though he slay me, I will approach him. I will lay my thoughts before him.

What did your children mean to you?
What was the gift that they brought to your life?
What was precious about each moment of every day?

My sons and daughters are at their feast! There is roast meat on the spit and there is a table with an abundance of the finest food! There is talk and there is laughter! They are seated in a circle as they tell their stories! Jemima, our second child, is speaking, our first daughter! Let me tell you of a time when I questioned Father closely. It was a time when I was quite young. Mattan had teased me by saying that he would go out on the caravans ... As she speaks, she adjusts her hood, which has blown across her face! A slight breeze is blowing towards the house from the wilderness! Noach helps her to adjust her hood and she continues to speak!

In famine, God shall redeem thee from death.
In war, from the power of the sword.

We hope.

Double to win. Double to win.
This is my motto. Double to win.
The size of your fortune shows what you have been.
This is my motto. Double to win.

Zophar's second speech. Why was he not content with berating me the first time? I can barely keep my mind on what he is saying.
Does Zophar say these things to everyone who suffers setbacks and disappointments? To one who loses a lamb? To one who misplaces a coin? To one who skins a knee? To one who breaks a fingernail?

A young boy, in the darkness - arranges the wood for a sacrifice - brigands along the way - my heart is like wax - thou crownest the year with thy goodness - make a joyful noise unto the lord - smashed against castle walls - to be pointing to something further - roots through the remnants - father of the fatherless.

"Knowest thou not this of old, since man was placed upon earth, that the triumphing of the wicked is short, and the joy of the hypocrite but for a moment? Though his excellency mount up to the heavens, and his head reach unto the clouds, yet he shall perish for ever like his own dung. They which have seen him shall say, Where is he? He shall fly away as a dream, and shall not be found: yea, he shall be chased away as a vision of the night. He hath swallowed down riches, and he shall vomit them up again. God shall cast them out of his belly. He shall suck the poison of asps: the viper's tongue shall slay him. He shall not see the rivers, the floods, the brooks of honey and butter. That which he laboured for shall he restore, and shall not swallow it down: according to his substance shall the restitution be, and he shall not rejoice therein; because he hath oppressed and hath forsaken the poor; because he hath violently taken away an house which he builded not. When he is about to fill his belly, God shall cast the fury of his wrath upon him, and shall rain it upon him while he is eating. He shall flee from the iron weapon, and the bow of steel shall strike him through. The heaven shall reveal his iniquity, and the earth shall rise up against him. The increase of his house shall depart, and his goods shall flow away in the day of his wrath. This is the portion of a wicked man from God, and the heritage appointed unto him by God."

O Lord, thou hast searched mee, and knowen me.
Thou knowest my downe sitting, and mine vprising: thou vnderstandest my thought afarre off.

My sons and daughters are at their feast! They all sit in a circle! The servants replenish their wine as they sit and talk! Our children's children sit and listen at their parents' feet! The breeze has become a wind, but the sun is still bright! Heber, our third child, is speaking, our second son! Let me tell you of a time, when I faced a difficult decision. There was a widow who had six fields. Sunlit hillsides, sparkling rivulets, grazing sheep ... Heber pauses as he speaks! Noach holds up his knife and it gleams in the light! Let us continue, he says to Heber! We can have no doubt that the day will continue to please!

Thou shalt be in league with the stones of the field.
And the beasts of the fields will be at peace with thee.

We fear.

I reach my leaves towards the sky but I never get there.
I stretch my roots towards the centre of the earth but I never get there.
I wonder what it is to be a tree.

Many years ago. When Eliphaz and I were both young men.
Meeting my good friend, Eliphaz, at the well.
Six day's journey from the land of Tirzah. The camels and the donkeys covered in dust. His handlers drawing water for the beasts of burden. Eliphaz with a dipper, slaking his thirst. And how was your journey, my good friend Eliphaz? How was the surface of the road? Were there brigands along the way? Was there water enough for your animals? His face is beaming; he seems distracted; he hardly seems to hear my words. I have good news to share with you, Job! You are my closest friend and I wish to tell you first! Do you recall the eldest daughter of our good friend, Baruch? We met her as we were talking beside the well! I have been fond of her since that day! She was bare-foot and wearing an earth-coloured robe! While visiting Baruch this time, I took the opportunity to ask for her hand in marriage! I am sure she has better prospects, but, to keep the story short, Baruch accepted me! Why, what is the

matter, Job? Do you not share in my elation? Can you not wish your closest friend all the best in his future life? Can you not wish me children and grandchildren and a long and prosperous existence? I am elated! I am distracted! I am amazed at my good fortune! Job, this is a great and glorious day!

Counting my sheep, my camels and my oxen.
Trying to speak the thing that is right.
Growing old with my wife and all of our children.

"Did you give my note to Baruch?"

"Most certainly, my old friend! Would I fail my old friend, Job? I delivered your note promptly, as you asked me to do!"

"Did he open it while you were there, in his presence? Did he share its contents with you? What did he say?"

Have not whole armies been destroyed in a single day?
Have not women been repeatedly raped on battlefields?
Have babies' skulls not been smashed against castle walls?

My sons and daughters are at their feast! The day is losing its brightness! Clouds are gathering over their heads! Epher, our fourth child, is speaking! Our third son! Let me tell you of a time when Father and I were in a caravan, and a sandstorm blew up from out of the desert. Father asked me if I would feel safe if I rode alone ... Epher pauses and looks at the sky! A servant fills Epher's cup and the others hold out their cups and they are topped up one by one! Epher turns toward Noach! Do you think it would be better if we moved inside?

The mountains are always there. Wrapped in a blanket of snow. Hidden behind a veil of swirling mist.

And God blessed them, saying, Be fruitfull, and multiply, and fill the waters in the Seas, and let foule multiply in the earth.

I seem to dream of stream-beds where the rocks are powder-dry, and of fields given over to thorns, and of skeleton-like goats who pull up clumps of grasses, dead to the roots.

My sons and daughters are at their feast! The sky is dull! The faces grow dim! It is harder to see! Bazak, our fifth child, is speaking! Our fourth son! Let me tell you of a time when I spoke to Father. I had heard stories of a land wherein all was prosperous. The river overflowed in the spring and replenished the soil. It was a land were all things were possible, and they had no droughts or monsoons, and I wondered whether I should just get up and go there ... Noach holds up his knife and it gleams quite dully! There is very little shine on it at all! Noach frowns as Bazak's story rattles on!

At destruction and famine shalt thou laugh.
Nor shalt thou be afraid of the demons of the earth.

We rejoice.

You say that you want to talk, my son.
Though silence was golden before.
It is words that leave the deepest wounds.
I would rather you use a knife.

Kezia, our second daughter. Kezia, our beautiful daughter. Kezia, our accomplished one.

A number of years ago. A fine spring day. A chat by the well.

She fills the jugs for the daughters of the village. I stand in the shade and watch them as they laugh and chirp and chatter in the sunshine beside the well. They are all young and cheerful, optimistic and free from care. Kezia talks to each as she fills each young girl's jug. A word of kindness for one, a compliment for another, a word of motherly advice for a girl only a few years younger than herself. Each girl basks in the radiance of our second daughter's smile. She is Kezia, our second daughter, the girl whom every one praises. Your daughter is such a treasure. Your daughter is so lovely. Your daughter is so gentle and sweet and kind. But Kezia has a problem. She has come to marriage age. She is troubled by her good fortune. It is not always pleasant to be so blessed. Her mother is aware of her brooding, her silent moments, her quiet sighs. Perhaps we two are the only ones who have noticed these weighty cares. Everyone else is aware of her smile, her cheerful chatter and her kindly ways. The girls are all gone now, with their jugs of water on their shoulders. I approach as Kezia, our daughter, pulls the rope and draws her water from the well.

Precisely and strategically - guesses at truth - a land wherein all was prosperous - I am become a stranger - a thousand years in thy sight - the ruthless reiteration of traditional beliefs - leave the deepest wounds - trembling hands and failing eyes - i am weary of my crying - a tree grew in the forest.

"You are fortunate, my daughter. I am sure that you will make a wise choice. You realize, I know, that marriage is for life."

"I know that, Father. But it is so difficult to choose. Could you and Mother not help me to make up my mind?"

"It is a burden to be so desirable. To have two suitors who desire your hand. Many there are who have no choice to make at all."

A village chanting psalms around a campfire.
The departure of a group of friends.
Hands reaching out to close a shutter.

My sons and daughters are at their feast! The sky is darkening rapidly! The children nestle into their mothers' robes! The servants are placing stones on the table to hold the tablecloth down! Kezia, our sixth child, is speaking, our second daughter! Let me tell you of the time when I had two suitors. Of the time when I spoke to Father beside the well ... She has barely started when the wind becomes a howl! Plates and cups blow off the table! Noach holds up his knife! The sky is darkening, he says! See, there is not a gleam in the knife! There are many more stories to tell! Forgive me for interrupting, Kezia, but you can continue your story of the suitors inside the house! Evron, Avram and Keren will surely have stories to tell! Let us quickly hustle inside! When it is my turn, I shall tell the story of Father and my knife!

Thou compassest my path, and my lying downe, and art acquainted with all my wayes.
For there is not a worde in my tongue: but lo, O Lord, thou knowest it altogether.

We mourn.

Finding the place where wisdom is to be found.
Setting an end to darkness.
Reasoning with those whom I have made.

Must I reply to Zophar's second speech? How many more such speeches is he planning to make?
The outfitters ready the caravans. The shepherds drive their sheep into the pens. Oh to be sizing up the arrivals in the marketplace.
By what authority has he spoken? Has Zophar suffered from painful boils? Has he suffered from fever and pain? Has he lost all ten of his children? Been an outcast from his tribe? My throat is as dry as a river-bed. My skin is a blanket of fire. I refrain from scratching the open sores on my face. It is agony to summon up my words.

A young shepherd went to see his wise friend.
I would be grateful if you would provide me with further advice.
The wise friend repeated what he had said before.
If ever you are menaced by a fierce wolf, reach out and stroke him under the chin.

He will become placid. Almost a friend.
All experience is one experience, repeating endlessly.
Self-evident for those with eyes to see.
This is the only advice that you will ever need.

"Wherefore do the wicked live, become old, yea, are mighty in power? Their seed is established in their sight with them, and their offspring before their eyes. Their houses are safe from fear, neither is the rod of God upon them. Their bull gendereth, and faileth not; their cow calveth, and casteth not her calf. They send forth their little ones like a flock, and their children dance. They take the timbrel and harp, and rejoice at the sound of the organ. They spend their days in wealth, and in a moment go down to the grave. How oft is the candle of the wicked put out! And how oft cometh their destruction upon them! God distributeth sorrows in his anger. Shall any teach God knowledge? Seeing he judgeth those that are high. One dieth in his full strength, being wholly at ease and quiet. His breasts are full of milk, and his bones are moistened with marrow. And another dieth in the bitterness of his soul, and never eateth with pleasure. They shall lie down alike in the dust, and the worms shall cover them. How then comfort ye me in vain, seeing in your answers there remaineth falsehood?"

Blow against the embers - deepens in intensity and pitilessness - in fear of every footstep - no news of barachel - growing old and full of days - blotted out of the book of the living - a gaggle of giggling geese - the hunted creature he feels himself to be - equal to my calamity - I am poor and needy.

My sons and daughters are at their feast! They are muffling up in their robes and moving towards their brother's house! Noach is holding the door open and waving them inside! The men are helping the servants to gather up the wine bottles and the glasses and whatever food they can carry and they smile as they hustle into their brother's house! The girls are chuckling as they wrestle with their hair and their hoods! They shoo their children in before them like a gaggle of giggling geese! I try to follow them in but I cannot move! His youngest one is clutching Noach's hand! Noach scoops the little one up in his arms and glances up at the sky and then ducks inside! Mattan pulls the door shut and, one by one, many hands reach out and the shutters are pulled around on their hinges and secured! Why can I not call out to them? Why can I not go with them inside! All of my children and my children's children have gone into the house!

A man carrying tablets down a mountain. A man in fear of every footstep. A man who hesitates when he hears a discordant sound.

A man fetching water for a young girl.
A wife who brings water and food to eat.

Tracking wastes in the face of blinding sand.

The sound of singing. The sound of dancing. A golden calf.

Thou hast beset me behind, and before: and laid thine hand vpon me.
Such knowledge is too wonderfull for me: it is high, I cannot attaine vnto it.

What can he do to make things right? What to do in this situation? What will his god say of the things that he might do?

What would Barachel be saying if he were sitting here on the ash-heap and speaking to me in Zophar's place?

What sort of hedge was about your children?
From what did your god protect them?
From what did your god protect them if not from life?

We pray.

My sons and daughters are at their feast! They are inside my son's house! A great wind is coming from the wilderness! It is shaking the four corners of the house! The sky is so dark it is black! A shutter is torn loose and bangs in the gale! A hand reaches out and pulls it shut! Mattan! Is that you? Noach! Can you hear me? They will fasten the shutters from the inside! They will put a big bar on the door! The house is shaking! The roof will fall in! All of my children are inside! Mattan! Jemima! Heber! Epher! Bazak! Kezia! Evron! Avram! Noach! Karen! Why can I not pummel on the door and save your lives?

Chapter 11

Five of us on the ash-heap. The third speech of Eliphaz.
Two men meeting a young girl at a well.
By what authority does Eliphaz speak? Who does he know who has suffered as I? What has happened in his own life that would be equal to my calamity? He is covered in dust and ashes, but has he earned them with the pain of his skin?

My skin is on fire. My life is in ashes. My children are dead.

Let the day perish wherein I was born, and the night in which it was said there is a man child conceived.

A son returning home to a waiting father.
Travellers muffled up in the midst of a sandstorm.
A man who dreams about a little boy.

Let that day be darkness, let not God regard if from above, neither let the light shine upon it.

Dying, after growing old and full of days.
Talking with a friend at the lagoon.
Making an offering of bullocks and rams to the lord.

Let darkness and the shadow of death stain it, let a cloud dwell upon it, let the blackness of the day terrify it.

Why do you fear the onset of dreams?
Do your dreams not speak to you?
What is it that you are so afraid to hear?

Five of us on the ash-heap. The third speech of Eliphaz.

A young girl in an earth-coloured robe with bare feet.

Why do my so-called friends attack me? Why do they think that the topic of my words is me? Who do they think I wish to talk to? Who do they think I wish to hear? Where does their wisdom come from? Of what is it made?

God maketh small the drops of water.
Which the clouds do drop and distill upon man abundantly.

We laugh.

A tree grows in the forest.
A bough grows in the shade; the leaves seek the sun.
The leaves whisper as the bough moves.
Am I the master here or are you?

Eliphaz is speaking. A third speech if you please.

The scall has spread after my cleansing. The priest looked in on me. The priest found yellow hair. I am unclean.

No matter that Job is suffering. Eliphaz is speaking! All of the hills are listening! The mountains attend!

Psalms of elation and sadness - to make us feel the triple contrast - I will hope continually - we pray, we affirm, we endure - my skin is on fire - the wrestling of an individual soul - aware of your every gesture - like rain upon the mown grass - am I the master here - a long and difficult journey.

"Is not thy wickedness great? And thine iniquities infinite? For thou hast taken a pledge from thy brother for nought, and stripped the naked of their clothing. Thou hast not given water to the weary to drink, and thou hast withholden bread from the hungry. Is not God in the height of heaven? And behold the height of the stars, how high they are! And thou sayest, How doth God know? Can he judge through the dark cloud? Thick clouds are a covering to him that he seeth not; and he walketh in the circuit of heaven. Acquaint now thyself with him, and be at peace: thereby good shall come unto thee. Receive, I pray thee, the law from his mouth, and lay up his words in thine heart. If thou return to the Almighty, thou shalt be built up, thou shalt put away iniquity. For then shalt thou have thy delight in the Almighty, and shalt lift up thy face unto God. Thou shalt make thy prayer unto him, and he shall hear thee, and thou shalt pay thy vows. Thou shalt also decree a thing, and it shall be established unto thee: and the light shall shine upon thy ways."

It is a good thing to giue thanks vnto the Lord, and to sing praises vnto thy Name, O most High.

To shew foorth thy louing kindnesse in the morning: and thy faithfulnesse euery night.

Five of us on the ash-heap. The third speech of Eliphaz.

A young man filling a water jug for a girl.

I believe that I shall faint. The sun is hot and my throat is dry. The flies are buzzing on the ash-heap. A stray dog roots through the remnants of someone's meal. I can barely see Eliphaz; I can barely hear.

God's eyes are upon the ways of man.
He sees all their goings.

We cry.

A man was alone on the desert.
He cursed his vile luck.
I am a brackish oasis, he said to himself.
There are no people here for me to poison.

Bildad and I as partners. Many years ago.

Bildad sitting on the ground. A broken man dissolved in tears. Sitting in the dust and telling his story.

I sold the grain at twice the price. I could have sold it for even more. The bidding raged on fiercely. They were desperate to have the grain. Their beasts were dying in the fields, Job. They had gone for months without rain. I sold the mules as well, Job, and that for a good price too. Then our drivers and I settled down to spend the night. But something terrible happened. While we were sleeping, everything changed. A rumour spread throughout the city. Some of their animals were getting sick. They claimed that the grain that I had sold them contained a blight. They became an angry mob. They dragged me to the market-place. They threatened to take my life. Word spread throughout the area. More and more buyers began to appear. They all demanded their money back. There was nothing I could do, Job. I was forced to give back the money that we had made on the sale of the grain. I was lucky to escape with my life. Our drivers were terrified. I had to save their lives. People were dumping our grain on the ash-heap. They were setting it alight. They blamed us for introducing a blight to their crops. I had no choice in the matter, Job. You would have had to do the same. I had to give back the money for all of the grain.

Laying upon man no more than right.
Returning to the days of my youth.
Breaking mighty men into pieces.

"Did you find out which grain was blighted? Did you tell them whose it was? Did you not keep the money for the healthy grain?"

"How was I to tell? There was no knowing which grain was blighted! I kept no records of who had bought each bag of grain!"

"You should have kept my money! I sent no blighted grain! Did you check your grain carefully before you loaded it on your mules? You sold your blighted grain along with mine!"

Why do we chant the ancient words?
Did the ancients know more than we know?
Why have these ancient notions come down to us through the years?

Five of us on the ash-heap. The third speech of Eliphaz.
A young man toiling endlessly with a dream in his mind.
How can some people talk so long with so little to say? It is flinging words at the darkness. A dog can bark all night and his throat will not be sore.

The desert sands are always shifting. Covering up the tracks of loved-ones. Revealing ancient inscriptions which were chiseled by living hands.

And God said, Let the earth bring forth the liuing creature after his kinde, cattell, and creeping thing, and beast of the earth after his kinde: and it was so.

The little boy again. He has been here every day.
Scraps of food in a wooden bowl and a pitcher from which he pours water into our flask as we eat. I pass the bowl around the circle and take mine last.
Is he bringing his own food? Is he denying himself for us? Who is it who has sent this boy to us?

Five of us on the ash-heap. The third speech of Eliphaz.
A young man sending a note along with a friend.
Oh why should I listen to Eliphaz? I have heard these words all my life. These are the things that people say. These are the sentiments that they exchange when they have no knowledge. Just once, I would like to turn things around; all of the humans would sit in silence; the voice of God would be the only voice that is heard.

God giveth rain upon the fields.

He sendeth waters upon the fields.

We wonder.

The cobbler examines his sandals in the marketplace.
He has used the finest leather, the finest thread.
He discovers why the sandals have failed to endure.
Each of their owners has been walking a crooked path.

We ride silently along, Evron and I.

Evron, our fifth son. Quiet now and staring straight ahead. Not a word have we spoken since we started home. Two donkeys and two masters, side by side.

Evron and I, in the fields with the sheep and the dogs and the shepherds. A commotion at the edge of the trail. Two shepherds stand and peer over the side. Evron and I walk over. A lamb, caught on a ledge, down below us. Lying on his side and bleating pitifully. Neither of the shepherds has made a move to attempt a rescue. They are waiting to see if the lamb will stand up and move. Evron gets down on his knees and looks over the side and turns to me. He is injured, Father. He is afraid. Can I go get him? The shepherds look at me and I shake my head. Evron has such compassion for the bleating lamb that I say, My son and I will go. We will see to the injured lamb. Evron and I make our way down to the rocky ledge. The sound of bleating is in our ears. Me first, Evron descending next. I pick my footing carefully and guide his sandals, one by one, in the safest footing. Slowly we reach the ledge. The lamb lies helplessly, bleating and looking up at us. Evron kneels down beside him and so do I. A quick examination with my fingers along the spine tells the tale, although I knew it before we descended. Otherwise, he would have been standing on the ledge rather than lying on his side all this time. His back is broken, Evron. He will never walk again. If we had left him here, he would have starved to death or been eaten by the wolves. We must put him out of his misery. Do you wish to do so, Evron? His face is stricken. No? Then I will do it. Do you wish to look the other way? I find a suitable rock and the deed is quickly done. The climb back up is slow, but we accomplish it. The rest of the day is spent in total silence between myself and Evron. I speak to the shepherds and they speak to me. If spoken to, Evron responds, but otherwise he doesn't speak at all. We finally say goodbye to the shepherds and are on our way. And now, we ride in silence towards our home.

The soul of the turtledove - going to and fro in the earth - the height of the stars - it never got there - takes a different direction - stricken down by an immense woe - alone on the desert - the waters of a full cup - eager for the killing - as you make your way.

"About another hour's ride. We'll soon be home."
"Yes, Father."

"We'll wash the dust from our feet. We'll have a good meal."

A man who shares his elation with a friend.
A messenger bringing news of a great loss.
An injured man riding on a donkey.

Five of us on the ash-heap. The third speech of Eliphaz.
A young man handing a note to an older man.
Eliphaz is speaking, but I can't seem to concentrate on his words. Oh Eliphaz. I am in agony from my boils. I am in agony and you are my torturer. I am in pain and you bring me no balm. My skin crawls. My ears buzz. There is no water in the jar. Why have you come to see me? You should have shrugged when you heard of my troubles. There is no one more easily forgotten than a former friend.

Upon an instrument of tenne strings, and vpon the psalterie: vpon the harpe with a solemne sound.
For thou, Lord, hast made me glad through thy worke: I will triumph in the workes of thy hands.

We doubt.

Looking up at the stars.
Drinking cold water on a hot day.
Tightening the cinch on a mule.

Eliphaz completes his third speech and sits with a smug look on his face.
This is the Eliphaz who has brought such pain to my life.
My difference is not with Eliphaz. Nor with Bildad nor with Zophar. The speaker I would like to hear is God. Why does God not speak to me? Why does God not listen to me? Why does God himself not come to this ash-heap and speak? I make an inner-shrug; I brace myself; I gather my thoughts. I look Eliphaz square in the face and begin to talk.

An elder brother spoke in jest to his younger brother.
My inheritance to you for a mess of pottage.
I will put my word in writing – in the air.

"Even today is my complaint bitter. My stroke is heavier than my groaning. Oh that I knew where I might find him! That I might come even to his seat! I would order my cause before him, and fill my mouth with arguments. I would know the words which he would answer me, and understand what he would say unto me. Behold, I go forward, but he is not there; and backward, but I cannot perceive him: On the left hand, where he doth work, but I cannot behold him: he hideth himself on the right hand, that I cannot see him; but he knoweth the way that I take: when he hath tried me, I shall come forth as gold. My foot hath held his steps, his way have I kept, and not declined. Neither have I gone back from the commandment of his lips; I have esteemed the words of his mouth more than my necessary food. But he is in one mind, and who can turn him? And what his soul desireth, even that he doeth."

A man on hands and knees - the life of the village - something terrible happened - the earth and all the inhabitants thereof - the beliefs in which he had been brought up - departure of my friends - scraps of food in a wooden bowl - brought terror when men craved for comfort - the world that i have made - i have considered the days of old.

Five of us on the ash-heap. The third speech of Eliphaz.
A bare-foot girl in a brightly-coloured robe.
Why does my wife say so little? Why did Barachel not send word? Why does the boy never speak, though he comes each day? No more, please, Eliphaz. Why must you speak on behalf of God? Why must you plague me with your ever-relentless words? Why can you not sit on the ash-heap in silence and share my grief?

A man with his son on an altar. A man who has tied up his son. A man who arranges the wood for a sacrifice.

Fingers searching underneath a coat of wool.
A daughter who questions her father closely.
The way of the camel and the way of the sheep.

Looking into his son's eyes. Looking into the eyes of his son. Looking into the eyes of his precious son.

O Lord, how great are thy workes! and thy thoughts are very deepe.
A brutish man knoweth not: neither doeth a foole vnderstand this.

A man who picks up a knife. A man who approaches his son. A man who raises his knife and says a prayer.

Would that Barachel were here. We made a solemn pact. We agreed to be bound together for the rest of our lives.
We have had no contact over the years, except for messages of good will and pledges of our friendship by way of infrequent travellers. I never again passed through Barachel's land and Barachel has never plied the trade routes at all.

A pity we have not met since. I always think of him as the one who shares my thoughts.

What do our ancient stories tell us?
What is disclosed to us in our dreams?
Are not the greatest truths revealed in our daily lives?

We affirm.

Five of us on the ash-heap. The third speech of Eliphaz.
A young man asking questions at a wedding.
What if God were to come and talk to me? What is it that he would say? Would he say what these human have said to me? Would he echo their very words? Surely God would not speak the words of my so-called friends. Surely the wisdom of man cannot be the wisdom of God.

Chapter 12

God is standing in a courtyard! He seems to be waiting for something to happen! He is standing in a courtyard and waiting for something to happen or for someone to arrive! Now, a messenger appears and speaks to God! The sons of God have come to present themselves to you, here in heaven. Will you see them now, my Lord, or would you prefer another time? God replies to the messenger! Bring them forth. I will see them now. I am anxious to hear the latest report from the world that I have made.

As for the night of my birth, let darkness seize upon it, let it not be joined unto the days of the year, let it not come into the number of the months.

Twelve people in the glow of a crackling fire.
A little boy who never answers and never speaks.
A father who gives his son a choice.

Let that night be solitary. Let no joyful voice come therein.

Overturning nations by the roots.
Being eyes for the blind.
Begetting the drops of dew.

Let them curse it that curse the day, who are ready to raise up their mourning.

Why do you seek God in heaven?
Is he not present on the earth?
Is he not all around you as you live and breathe?

A courtyard in heaven! God is standing in the centre! A messenger motions and a group of figures moves into the courtyard and stands in a circle around God! One of them steps forward! I cannot believe my eyes! It seems to be a second God! How can this be! This personage looks exactly like God himself! I look from God to God! I look and look again at the second God and cannot believe that he looks exactly like God himself! How can this be true? How can there be two of God? This is impossible! Surely the first God is God and the second God is merely a messenger! One of the sons of heaven! The Eye of God or some such other personage who reports to God of the doings in the world that he has made!

God will not caste out a perfect man.
He will fill thy mouth with laughing and thy lips with rejoicing.

We flourish.

A man on hands and knees in the burning sand.
Hungry, thirsty, desperate.
Acutely aware of the flapping of wings above his head.
The shadow of the bird blots out his own.

Bildad is speaking. This is his third speech. Was there not enough condemnation in the first two speeches?

My mind wanders far away from what he is saying.

How long has he waited for the moment when I would be cornered and helpless like this? Days? Weeks? Years? Was he ever my friend, or did he look for my comeuppance from the very beginning? Well, if to scourge me is his wish, he has me helpless. I am in pain, my strength is gone, I have no stamina to speak of. I am helpless to parry the blows that I know will descend.

The words of my roaring - man did eat angels' food - the world that I have made -
all the elements in this varied world - a statement of fact - blood they have shed like water -
being eyes for the blind - his thought trembles at the hidden considerations - close to a
seamless mend - a long trek over difficult terrain.

"Dominion and fear are with him, he maketh peace in his high places. Is there any number of his armies? And upon whom doth not his light arise? How then can man be justified with God? Or how can he be clean that is born of a woman? Behold even to the moon, and it shineth not; yea, the stars are not pure in his sight. How much less man, that is a worm? And the son of man, which is a worm?"

Praise ye the Lord. Praise God in his Sanctuarie: Praise him in the firmament of his
power.
Praise him for his mightie actes: Praise him according to his excellent greatnesse.

A courtyard in heaven! There are two who look like God! The first God asks the second God, Whence comest thou? The second God answers the first God and says, From going to and fro in the earth and from walking up and down in it. The first God then asks the second God, Hast thou considered our servant Job, that there is none like him in the earth, a perfect and an upright man, one that feareth God, and escheweth evil? Then the second God answers the first God and says, Doth Job fear God for nought? Hast not thou made an hedge about him, and about his house, and about all that he hath on every side? Thou hast blessed the work of his hands, and his substance is increased in the land. But put forth thine hand now, and touch all that he hath, and he will curse thee to thy face. And the first God says to the second God, Behold, all that he hath is in thy power; only upon himself put not forth thine hand.

To fear the Lord is wisdom.
Evil is understanding.

We falter.

A behemoth looked a leviathan in the eye.
I contribute more than you to life on the earth.
When I have time I am going to make a list.

Zophar and I. When we were young and sharing our dreams.

My annual spring trip to visit my flock. My donkey seems so slow. Apprehension as I make my way along the trail to the land of the Naahamites.

What to do about my agreement with Zophar? What if my lambs are not hale and healthy? What if his lambs are superior to mine? How could such a thing have happened? Why the agreement that we made? I buy the sheep from him. My lambs are born in the spring. His men gather them in the pens. His men mark them with a nick in each ear. How could I have made such an agreement with a man I had hardly known? I was eager to start my flock. I had money enough to buy sheep, but I had no meadow to graze them in. Why did I agree to share my dream with him? Is he selling defective sheep? Is he marking them in his favour? Is he culling out the best lambs to mark as his own? To what field could I move my flock if I break the agreement? How could I look myself in the eye if I went back on my word? I do not know what I will do if my lambs are defective. I arrive at Zophar's meadow. Trickling water, green grass, a gentle breeze. Zophar strides across the field as I tie up my donkey. He neither smiles nor frowns. I strain to read the message in his eyes.

Dwelling in the land of Uz.
Enjoying the lush grass in my fields.
Remembering the day I met my wife.

"You say that you can afford a dozen more sheep, Job. Pick the best from among my flock. I will sell you my best rams and my best ewes for the price that you would pay for the poorest ones."

"Why are your lambs always so healthy and mine so poor? My lambs are smaller, feebler, punyer. What would cause some lambs to be healthy and others so poor?"

"Select the healthiest rams and ewes, Job. Take the best that I have in my flock. Sever them from the rest and mark them yourself."

Is God not aware of your every gesture?
Does God not hear your every word?
Does God not know your thoughts before even you are aware?

A courtyard in heaven! There are two who look like God! The second God speaks to the first God, As we are speaking, Job's oxen are plowing and his asses are feeding beside them. And the Sabeans are falling upon them and taking them away and slaying Job's servants with the edge of the sword. Only one messenger is escaping alone to tell him. The first God speaks to the second God, You have done well. You have kept within the bounds of our agreement. And the second God replies, There is more. As we are speaking, the fire of God is falling from heaven and is burning up Job's sheep and his servants and is consuming them. Only one of Job's servants is escaping alone to tell him. Then the first God speaks to the second God, You have done well. You have kept within the bounds of our agreement. And the second God replies, There is more. As we are speaking, the Chaldeans are making out three bands and are falling upon Job's camels and are carrying them away, yea, and are slaying Job's servants with the edge of the sword. Only one of Job's servants is escaping alone to tell him.

A wadi is never the same. An inviting apparition when seen in the distance. A heart-breaking mirage when closely approached.

And God said, Let vs make man in our Image, after our likenesse: and let them haue dominion ouer the fish of the sea, and ouer the foule of the aire, and ouer the cattell, and ouer all the earth, and ouer euery creeping thing that creepeth vpon the earth.

Rain clouds hover over the desert for what seem like weeks and weeks, while my camels scour the creek-beds, desperate for drink, and then they lie down on the dry rocks and die.

This is what I dream of whenever I fall asleep. I try to stay awake as long as I can.

A courtyard in heaven! There are two who look like God! Again there comes a day when the sons of God come to present themselves before God and a second God comes again among them to present himself before the first God! And the first God says to the second God, From whence comest thou? And the second God answers the first God and says, From going to and fro in the earth, and from walking up and down in it. And the first God says to the second God, Hast thou considered our servant Job, that there is none like him in the earth, a perfect and an upright man, one that feareth God, and escheweth evil? And still he holdeth fast his integrity, although thou movedst me against him, to destroy him without cause. And the second God answers the first God and says, Skin for skin, yea, all that a man hath will he give for his life. But put forth thine hand now, and touch his bone and his flesh, and he will curse thee to thy face. And the first God says to the second God, Behold, he is in thine hand; but save his life.

He breaks mighty men in pieces.
He sets others in their stead.

We gain.

A mule and a human rode along.
If humans were mules said the man,
We mules would gladly eat only half the feed.
If only God would hear and make this change.

A lion is coughing in the thicket.
It was wounded in a skirmish as the sun went down.
It is dark and we are sitting around the campfire waiting for dawn. The dogs whine and yelp at the darkness. They too wait for dawn. Avram, our sixth son, has spent the night with the hunters. They are hardening their spear-points in the fire. They explain the lore of the hunter and the lore of the lions. The two go hand in hand. I have hunted in my time, but now I send the hunters out and remain with the shepherds and the flock. Avram, our sixth son, the son of Job, could have that privilege as well, if he should want it. Why should the owner's son go hunting? Why should he take the risk? Sure enough, as dawn begins to break, he approaches me. Father, may I go with the hunters? I have asked them to teach me their lore. They say that they will do so if you will agree. I resist the urge to ask him what his mother would venture to say. I look in his eyes in the glow of the fire and I nod my assent. A hunter gives our son a spear and the small group whispers in a cluster as they plot their siege. At dawn the thicket swallows them one by one. Time goes by as I warm my hands. The lion's cough is louder now. Perhaps the scent of the hunters has come to his nostrils. He is dying. He is fierce. He is lying in wait to pounce on his hated foe. Perhaps an unwary novice hunter will furnish him one last taste of blood before he is killed. Avram our sixth son. We have

seven sons and three daughters, but we have no children to spare. What will his mother say if I bring him home in a litter? What a display that would be. A lion and a boy lying side by side in the village square for all to see. The lion coughs again. Louder, it seems, than ever. The men and the boy who are hunting him make no sound. I turn back to the fire and warm my hands in the cool morning air.

I crie in the day time - a series of rhetorical questions - the message in his eyes - thou feedest with the bread of tears - to speak no words - my children are dead - considered our servant job - the sparrow hast found an house - our words rise up to the heavens - either beside the mark or cruelly unjust.

"Is the cough getting louder, would you say?"
"Lions are dangerous when they are hurt."
"It seems to be louder every time the old fellow coughs."

A grandfather telling a story to his grandchildren.
A barefoot girl with a water jug.
A fatted calf and flowing wine.

A courtyard in heaven! There are two who look like God! The second God is speaking to the first God, As we are speaking, Job is being smote with sore boils from the sole of his foot unto his crown. His boils are agonizing. His whole body is wracked with pain. If he sits, he wants to stand. If he stands, he wants to sit down. His skin is being pocked with running sores. His eyes are filling with rheum. No one knows him by his looks. He is shivering as he sits by the fire. He is burning as he stands in the breeze. He is in agony every second. Every breath he is taking he is hoping will be his last. He is taking a potsherd and scraping himself. Now, he is sitting himself down among the ashes.

Praise him with the sound of the Trumpet: Prayse him with the Psalterie and Harpe.
Praise him with the timbrell and dance: praise him with stringed instruments, and Organes.

We lose.

Renewing my bow in my hand.
Marking all the paths.
Causing the cry of the poor to come onto me.

Bildad ends his third speech. It is my turn to reply. Oh, what can I possibly say?

The tents flap in the breeze in the marketplace. Old men discuss the weather and the state of the crops.

Bildad is in love with his own wisdom. He is a worshipper of the self. He sits on our ash-heap as if he is speech-making from on top of a cloud. Nothing that he has said to me has justified his posing as a fount of wisdom. He has never had a thought in his life that wasn't chewed by other teeth before it came to him. He knows what I am thinking. I can see it in his eyes. I moisten my tongue and summon up my words.

All of the clouds were gathered together.
Every cloud on the earth in one big room.
Let us rain when there are humans in the desert.
Why waste the rainfall, waste the flowers, waste the bloom?

"How hast thou helped him that is without power? How savest thou the arm that hath no strength? How hast thou counselled him that hath no wisdom? And how hast thou plentifully declared the thing as it is? To whom hast thou uttered words? And whose spirit came from thee? Dead things are formed from under the waters, and the inhabitants thereof. Hell is naked before him, and destruction hath no covering. He stretcheth out the north over the empty place, and hangeth the earth upon nothing. He bindeth up the waters in his thick clouds, and the cloud is not rent under them. He holdeth back the face of his throne, and spreadeth his cloud upon it. He hath compassed the waters with bounds, until the day and night come to an end. The pillars of heaven tremble and are astonished at his reproof. He divideth the sea with his power, and by his understanding he smiteth through the proud. By his spirit he hath garnished the heavens; his hand hath formed the crooked serpent. Lo, these are parts of his ways: but how little a portion is heard of him? But the thunder of his power who can understand?"

Everyone chants in reply - earely will I seek thee - disarm them with idle chatter - naked came I - truth shall spring out of the earth - nothing but a sublime hymn - dawn of a terrible nightmare - broken down all his hedges - clinging to temporal things - never to deceive himself.

A courtyard in heaven! There are two who look like God! The first God speaks to the second God, In all of this, you have done well. You have kept within the bounds of our agreement. And the second God replies, But there is more. As we are speaking, Job's sons and his daughters are eating and drinking wine in their eldest brother's house. And, behold, there is coming a great wind from the wilderness and is smiting the four corners of the house. It is falling upon Job's family and they are dying. Job will soon be hearing the news. One servant is escaping alone to tell him.

An old man talking to his son. Asking him to come closer. Asking him which of his sons is he.

An assessment made when the winds have quieted down.
A wounded lion coughing in the dark.
A mob with clubs and pitchforks and spears.

The son asks the old man for a blessing. How can this be so? He has blessed and been kissed by his son not long ago.

Praise him vpon the loud cymbals: praise him vpon the high sounding cymbals.
Let euery thing that hath breath, praise the Lord..

The old man begins to tremble. The dawn of a terrible nightmare. His blessing has been given to the unrighteous son.

It was strange that the brigand took Barachel's word that I should be spared.

Could it be that Barachel was a brigand too? A fellow of the trade? Was brigandry his purpose in being on the road that day? To meet with travellers and disarm them with idle chatter – to probe their worth as prospective prey – until his fellow brigand should arrive to take their purses and perhaps their lives?

What if I had not saved Barachel's life that day?

Can God be known only in heaven?
Can God be known only in dreams?
Is God not as close to you as the hem of your sleeve?

We endure.

How can this be happening? Such terrible events! There are two who look like God! I look from God to God! I keep waiting for the first God to over-rule the second God! To tell him to stop what he is doing and to leave my family alone! Surely the first God doesn't actually intend that my family should be taken away from me! Surely he only means to test me! He means for the second God to hold his hand at the last minute and not sweep my children away to devastation! Who is this Second God? An Accuser? A Courtier? An Attendant? A Functionary? An Eye of God? A Satan? The two are standing behind an altar! I strain for a better look at the second God, but I cannot see his feet! Surely the windstorm is a warning! Why are these terrors not overruled? Why are these powers not being denied? Why does God not come to my rescue? Perhaps I have displeased him! Perhaps it is not too late! These things are happening as they talk! Perhaps this agreement can be reversed! There must be something I can do, or my children can do, that will stay the hand of God – whichever God is God – and spare the lives of my children whom I love!

Chapter 13

Four of us on the ash-heap. It will be Zophar's third speech. Must I resign myself to hearing his thoughts again?

A young man browsing in a market place.

Why do my friends insist on telling me how wrong I have been?

My skin is on fire. My life is in ashes. My children are dead.

Let the stars of the twilight be dark. Let it look for light but have none. Neither let it see the dawning of the day.

Two people thinking, though they seldom speak.
An old man with scar-tissue on his arms.
A man on an ash-heap yearning for his friend.

Because it shut up not the doors of my mother's womb, nor hid sorrow from mine eyes.

Holding my child's hand.
Mourning my lost children.
Suffering boils from my soles to my crown.

Why died I not from the womb? Why did I not give up the ghost when I came out of the belly?

Are we close to God in our thoughts?
Are we close to God in our prayers?
Are we close to God in our clinging to temporal things?

Only four of us on the ash-heap. Waiting for Zophar to arrive.

A young man buying sheep from his new-found friend.

But where is Zophar? The others have each spoken thrice. Zophar has only spoken twice. A Naamathite missing a chance to make a speech? Why is he not here? Why is he not telling me how right he is with his god? Why is he not condemning me for not living a life like he? A life that pleases God? That keeps him free from boils and puss and agony? That keeps his children free of collapsing buildings? He had better hurry or he will lose his chance to rail at me. The others, I am sure, would gladly take his place.

God discovereth deep things out of darkness.
He bringeth out to light the shadow of death.

We hope.

Double to win. Double to win.
This is my motto. Double to win.
The reward for a life that is free of all sin.
This is my motto. Double to win.

Where is Zophar? He is not on the ash-heap as he has been every day since he arrived here.

His servant says that he arose early and left his tent and has not returned.

I wander through the town asking for Zophar. The merchants and their wares. Pots and wineskins. Sandals and bridles. Meat and vegetables. I pause at every stall. They do not recognize me physically, but all, no doubt, are aware of who I am. I am scanned for signs of the plague. Answers come quickly so as to send me on my way. Many do not know Zophar by his name. Many know of him but do not know where to find him. Finally, there is one who has risen early and knows Zophar by his name and his beard and his robe.

The needs of my flocks - those who walk a straight path - the redemptive transformation of suffering - the doors of my mother's womb - before the mountains were brought forth - nothing here but void - we spend our years as a tale that is told - a life that pleases god - to look beyond the tragedy - what was he thinking.

"Do you know my friend, Zophar? I am wondering where he has gone. I would like to talk with him."

"I know of whom you speak. I saw him walking through the village at daybreak. He took the path towards the lagoon."

"Thank you kindly. Did he look troubled? I will seek him there."

O God, thou art my God, earely will I seeke thee: my soule thirsteth for thee, my flesh longeth for thee, in a drie and thirstie lande, where no water is.
To see thy power and thy glory, so as I haue seen thee in the Sanctuary.

Where is Zophar?
A pasture with lush grass and a sparkling spring.
I make my way through the village. Vendors cry, camels cough, donkeys bray. Children play among the stalls. I chase away a dog who sniffs at my rags. I leave the streets and take the path along by the brook. Why has Zophar not come today? Does he not know that I have come to depend on his presence? He need not make a speech. We need no exchange of views. We need not argue and bicker. God must laugh as he listens to our confabs. Four fools explaining God's actions. Four fools explaining God's thoughts. Four fools calling the other three fellows fools and speaking for God. Barachel was right to enjoin his son to speak no words.

God doth not pervert judgement.
He doth not prevent justice.

We fear.

Watch us for a while said the other trees.
Watch us drink, watch us eat, watch us breathe, watch us grow.
Then you will know what it is to be a tree.

Many years ago. When Eliphaz and I were both young men.
At the wedding of Eliphaz and the eldest daughter of Baruch.
A great table with food and wine. Eliphaz and all the Temanites. Baruch and all his clansmen. Toasts, speeches, prayers, music. Pulling Baruch aside after he has had his celebratory dance with his eldest daughter. She is wearing a multi-coloured robe and her feet are bare. Her face is radiant as I lead her father away. We go out through the granary doors and into the night. There is a bonfire with many people gathered around. Singing and laughter and idle chatter. Praise God for our good fortune! Have all of you had enough to eat? The table groans with the benefice of our fields! There is plenty of meat on the spit! If anyone here is still hungry, please let him indulge! The firelight flickers on Baruch's face as we stand and talk. This is a wonderful time for me. My wife is very pleased. One yearns to see the start of the next generation. One wishes to be able to pass on what one has learned. As one gets older, one begins to fear that one's labour might well be in vain. It is a time of celebration. A time of thanking God for his beneficence. And as for you, young man, I barely know what to say. Your note came as a surprise. I had given up on you. I assumed that your interests lay elsewhere. I had no idea that you had any intention of asking for my eldest daughter's hand.

Seeing under the whole heaven.
Opening the ears of men.
Saying to a prince thou are

"So sorry to have had to turn you away, but I never knew of your feelings or your plans. I have always admired your abilities. Of course, I am extremely pleased with my new son in law, Eliphaz, but I must admit – confidentially, between the two of us, alone – that my wife and I both had our eye on you."

"Did you notice the seal on the letter? Had it been opened, do you think? Is there any way that Eliphaz could have known what was written inside?"

"Job, my young friend, I cannot believe that you are asking me such questions. I was distracted as you can imagine. In my euphoria at the occasion, I paid no attention to such a thing as a seal on a letter. He almost forgot to give it to me. He had it tucked away in a travel-bag. Eliphaz made his offer before he remembered your note."

Why are we given roses and cherries?
Why are we given such wonderful children?
Why would God give such things and then take them away?

Where is Zophar? Where can he be?
A herd of sheep grazing silently on a hillside.
Making my way along the path that leads to the lagoon. The others were chattering about Zophar's absence. They offered to draw straws to determine who would take his place. When have they ever missed a chance to give a speech? Let them chatter; let them draw straws; let them vie to take his place. I will not be there to hear them. I would rather find Zophar and ask him what took him away.

The mountains are always there. The mountains never move. They growl from time to time but they never move.

So God created man in his owne Image, in the Image of God created hee him; male and female created hee them.

I would like to dream of a day when my children will all come back to me.
Maybe that has something to do with the little boy.

Where is Zophar? Where has he gone?
A young man with a pen of sickly lambs.

I arrive at the oasis and look around me. I don't see anyone at first. The waters are calm and the morning sun shines on the lagoon. A group of girls on the other side is wading in the shallow waters. Their feet are bare and they kick up splashes of water and laugh and tease. A group of invalids is lying on the grass. They have taken a healing bathe. Not one of them calls to me. Not one of them seems to know me. Surely there are some to whom I have been kind in days gone by.

God puts no trust in his servants.
He charges his angels with folly.

We rejoice.

I talked with my brother; I talked with my wife.
I talked with my daughter; I talked with my son.
It is words that leave the deepest wounds.
I will bleed for the rest of my life.

Noach is polishing the blade of his knife.
Noach, our seventh and youngest son.
He strokes it over and over with the emery bar. The knife is already much brighter than any knife that I have ever seen, but Noach works towards a standard of perfection that only he can see. He is that way with everything he touches. When he mends harness, it is as close to a seamless mend as can possibly be. When he packs a load for a mule or a camel, the sacks balance perfectly, and it is effortless for the beast to bear his burden. Difficult horses, camels or mules are placid for him. With people, Noach is the same. Inner rage remains calm in volatile people who are in his presence. It is a gift with no visible origin – not from his mother, nor from me, nor from his known ancestors. And now, he polishes his knife with the emery bar. Will the beast that receives the knife accept it with ease? Will the beast sink down to its knees – ox or goat or lamb – and wonder what unfelt device has been employed to slit its throat for the sacrifice? The mystery about Noach is that there is no mystery. What is bothering him is not a question. What demons haunt him does not occur. What will he meet that will test his resources is not a concern. If I were not his father, I might well ask whose son is this? Noach pauses in his polishing and takes a drink from his flask. What can I say?

Overseeing the preparations - the compass slips from my grasp - the desires of individual human beings - a drie and thirstie lande - like the horn of a unicorn - wiser that the fowls of heaven - what was god's plan - explaining god's thoughts - god's government of human affairs - the lord knoweth the thoughts of man.

"Your work is always superb, my son. All of your efforts gleam like your knife. Everything you touch has a brilliant sheen."

"Thank you, Father."

"It is not a compliment, my son. More an observation. A comment that I would call a statement of fact."

A man with a split lip and a sad story.
Servants putting stones on a tablecloth.
Visitors who arrive in a time of need.

Where is Zophar? I seek to know.
A young man arguing fiercely with another young man.

I look along the bank and he is there. I walk along the edge of the calm lagoon. We go back a long way together. We have been battling since the days when I raised my sheep in the meadow on his hillside. Much of our time on this earth has been shared. We have seen heartbreak and we have seen joy. We have competed and we have been friends. We have proffered and we have withheld. We have talked and we have been silent. I missed his presence this morning at the ash-heap.

Because thy louing kindnes is better then life: my lips shal praise thee.
Thus will I blesse thee, while I liue: I will lift vp my handes in thy Name.
My soule shall be satisfied as with marrow and fatnesse: and my mouth shall praise thee with ioyfull lips.

We mourn.

Being advised to curse God and die.
Putting a bridle on a camel.
Walking through the village at dawn.

Zophar is sitting under a tree, beside the waters.

The waters are calm and cool. No doubt the morning is the most soothing part of the day.

He looks up as I approach. He has been here since the sunrise. What could he have been thinking? Surely not every thought that he has is concerned with Job. About what topics has he come to brood? His wife and his children? His brothers and his sisters? His friends and acquaintances? He has given all of these up to visit me. I missed him this morning. It was Zophar's turn to pontificate. As wrong-headed as he has been, I missed his voice. He looks up but doesn't speak. His bare feet are dangling in the waters. As he turns and faces me, he swings his feet around on the grass and the drips cause tiny ripples in the lagoon.

A young shepherd was menaced by a fierce pack of wolves.
The wolves spread out and surrounded him.
The young shepherd remembered the advice of his wise friend.
If ever you are menaced by a fierce wolf, reach out and stroke him under the chin.
He will become placid. Almost a friend.
The wolves bared their fangs and growled and moved towards him menacingly.
There were at least a dozen wolves.
Oh, thought the young shepherd to himself, I wish that I had the company of my wise
friend.

"I wonder why you have not come to speak to me today."
"I have come to feel that there is nothing left to say."
"I was assuming that we would continue to rant and rave."

Five people sitting and talking - the breasts that i should suck - between the skull or
the skin - given roses and cherries - the problem of what a good man should do - let the
heavens rejoice and let the earth be glad - what unfelt device has been employed - from
heaven did the lord behold the earth - made of wood and brass - the answer that there is no
real answer.

Zophar and I at the oasis.
A young man with lambs which he cannot sell.
Zophar and I sitting and talking. The waters are very calm. We talk softly as we sit
and, eventually, we walk back together through the town. Girls are laughing at the well.
Vendors are hawking in the marketplace. Women are dickering over the vegetables as they
fill their baskets. I glance around, but I do not see the boy. So you intend to remain silent for
the rest of your stay here? Zophar considers and then he speaks. Only the pleasantries will I
take part in. My disputations have come to an end. What to say to this? If he had spoken on
God's behalf I could have railed at him. Well, I manage to say, you have given me enough.
You should return, now, to your family and your friends.

An old man at the end of a life. Worn and tired, subdued and sad. Brooding on a land
that is far away.

A young boy riding a camel in a sandstorm.
A man with scars on his face and a knife in his belt.
A distraught young man at the wedding of a friend.

A man who has loved his people. Who has always wanted to do what he thought was best. Who wanted always to be right in the eyes of his god.

When I remember thee vpon my bed, and meditate on thee in the night watches.
Because thou hast bene my helpe; therefore in the shadow of thy wings will I reioyce.

He lies down with a vision. A vision of a land. A vision of a promised land as he lies down to die.

What would have happened otherwise? What if I had not saved Barachel's life earlier that day?

Had you come to think that you had created your children?
Had you come to think that they were things that you owned?
Are we partners with God or is God in a world of his own?

We pray.

Five of us on the ash-heap.
A young man alone in a field with a tattered dream.
Zophar and I return. The others are sitting and waiting in the broken circle. I take my place, at the spot where I always sit, facing the market and the gates. Zophar takes his place as well. The others look quizzically at Zophar. Why has Zophar been missing? Where has he been? Why did I seek to find him? What have we talked about? What will Zophar have to say? What will I say to Zophar in reply? Perhaps they are eager to relate what they have talked about while we have been away. All of us in a circle. Five people on an ash-heap. Job, Eliphaz, Bildad, Zophar and Elihu. The day is pleasant. The sun is shining. The life of the village goes on in the distance. No one speaks.

Chapter 14

Lying on something soft! A wisp of cloud or fog! Wondering where I am! Listening for sounds! And what is this object which lies beside me? A compass, it would seem! I rise up and look around! Nothing but mist for miles and miles! Then what is holding me up? And why does this compass not sink through the fog and disappear? It is made of wood and brass and seems very old! I pick it up and it feels foreign to my hand! What is it that a compass does? It is used to circumscribe! But what can one circumscribe in the murk of a mist or a fog?

Why did my mother's knees not prevent me? Or why the breasts that I should suck?

A traveller trapped on a ledge with a broken leg.
A young man huddled with a group of hunters.
A boy with a wooden bowl and a water jug.

For now should I have lain still and been quiet. Then I should have slept. Then I had been at rest.

Searching out all perfection.
Weighing myself in an even balance.
Scattering the east wind upon the earth.

Wherefore is light given to him that is in misery? And life unto the bitter soul?

Has God placed you in the midst of chaos?
Has God placed you alone in a void?
Does God require of you that you are to make a world?

Why not create my own little world? It makes me chuckle to think of my task! I have no doubt that I could very easily do so if I should try! I am Job – known far and wide as a man who get things done! I have seven thousand sheep, three thousand camels, five hundred yoke of oxen and a large staff of servants, all ready to stir at my command! I have fields and valleys and hillsides! Hundreds of people eat from my hand! And all of this was not inherited from my father, not at all! Family pride has always prevented me from mentioning publically what a pittance my father's patrimony turned out to be! It was I – I, Job – who built what I have out of almost nothing! So the creation of another such world would be nothing to me! I have my wits and my good right arm and this handy ancient compass of wood and brass! I will circumscribe a world in which I can live!

The light of the wicked shall be put out.
And the spark of his fire shall not shine.

We laugh.

Two drops of water falling on a mountain side.
Each joins a different rivulet as it trickles through a meadow.
Neither knows of the other; neither thinks.
The thought of masters and servants never occurs.

Elihu begs leave to speak. His eyes are moist with his passion. His brow is furrowed with thought.

The three old friends are shocked at the lack of respect and decorum. He has not been invited to participate. He has spoken out on his own. What would his father say at his son – the representative of his father and his tribe – speaking at a gathering out of turn?

An extremely sincere young man. Chafing in his harness of deference to his elders. Ears that hear the staleness of old ideas. Eyes that see how threadbare are ancient ways. How can his elders babble on so? Can they actually believe their own words? Their speeches are worn to threads with the chaffing of the years. He has listened, he has thought and now he wishes to speak. Let a young man clear up the matter in a few choice words. I turn away from my friends. I nod towards the boy and he bows his head in return. He clears his throat and begins to share his thoughts.

Double to win - a shattered dream - endure rather than question - my own little world - would I have done the same - man's complete inability to affect god - puts forth his hand - wine that maketh glad the heart of man - a small voice spoke up - a traveller trapped on a ledge.

"I am young, and ye are very old; wherefore I was afraid, and durst not shew you mine opinion. I said, Days should speak, and multitude of years should teach wisdom. But there is a spirit in man and the inspiration of the Almighty giveth them understanding. Great men are not always wise: neither do the aged understand judgment. Therefore I said, Hearken to me; I also will shew mine opinion. Behold, I waited for your words; I gave ear to your reasons, whilst ye searched out what to say. Yea, I attended unto you, and, behold, there was none of you that convinced Job, or that answered his words: Wherefore, Job, I pray thee, hear my speeches, and hearken to all my words. The Spirit of God hath made me, and the breath of the Almighty hath given me life. I also am formed out of the clay. I will answer thee, that God is greater than man. Why dost thou strive against him? For he giveth not account of any of his matters. For God speaketh once, yea twice, yet man perceiveth it not. Let us choose to us judgment; let us know among ourselves what is good. For his eyes are upon the ways of man, and he seeth all his goings. For he will not lay upon man more than right; that he should enter into judgment with God. Look unto the heavens, and see; and behold the clouds which are higher than thou. Where is God my maker, who giveth songs in the night, who teacheth us more than the beasts of the earth, and maketh us wiser than the fowls of heaven? Remember that thou magnify his work, which men behold. Every man may see it; man may behold it afar off. Behold, God is great, and we know him not, neither can the number of his years be searched out. For he maketh small the drops of water: they pour down rain according to the vapour thereof, which the clouds do drop and distil upon man abundantly. God thundereth marvellously with his voice; great things doeth he, which we cannot comprehend. For he saith to the snow, Be thou on the earth; likewise to the small rain, and to the great rain of his strength. He sealeth up the hand of every man, that all men may know his work. Touching the Almighty, we cannot find him out: he is excellent in power, and in judgment, and in plenty of justice: he will not afflict. Men do therefore fear him: he respecteth not any that are wise of heart."

He that dwelleth in the secret place of the most high: shall abide vnder the shadow of the Almightie.
I will say of the Lord, He is my refuge, and my fortresse: my God, in him will I trust.

I am a man and man is a creator! He is capable of momentous things! He has logic, energy and enterprise, so all lies ready to answer briskly to his command! I have my wits; I have the compass; I have the will! I search for a spot where I can begin! Here, in this mist? Here on this rock? Here on this sand? Here on this ooze? Just let me get settled down and I can begin! There will be men and women and children! There will be rivers and grass and trees! There will be fields and paths and houses! There will be grains and game and birds! And the sun will shine on the people! And there will be peace and plenty to eat! And they will thank me and ask my blessing! And all will be well in this land of nurturing! Just let me find a place where I can begin! It has something to do with this compass, of that I am sure!

God puts forth his hand upon the rock.
He overturneth the mountains by the roots.

We cry.

A man was alone on the desert.
He blessed his new-found luck.
Another man was moving towards him.
The stranger was holding out a jug of water.

No more partnerships with Bildad.

Time goes by. I suffer in silence. I put my hand to the plough and my shoulder to the wheel. Mucking in an irrigation ditch; bringing a breach-birth calf to light; keeping one eye on the skies for rain as I toil in the fields. It takes a long time to shore-up my holdings. The major setback has crippled my plans. I had counted on the profit from the caravan of grain.

Wondering about Bildad and the story of the famine. At camel markets, at foreign granaries, at stops for water along the trails, I talk with strangers from that faraway land. Was there a famine which strangled the crops in the fields of your land? Do you remember the arrival of a traveller with a caravan of mules? Do you remember animals stricken by blighted grain? Occasionally a caravan will stop by on its way to or from the land of the Shuhites. Do you know Bildad, a man from your country? Did he have any setbacks while building his fields and his herds? Was there any time when he suffered a blight to his grain? The donkeys are fed and the camels are watered as we talk. Do you recall the time of the famine? When Bildad set out for foreign markets with a caravan of grain? Did he come home with his fortune diminished, do you remember, or did he emerge from that venture with a more than double gain? The traveller shakes his head. Bildad is the richest man in the district! The widow's saviour and the orphan's friend! Everything he touches seems to prosper in his hands! Occasionally Bildad comes through with a caravan – large or small – on his way to trade at a market in another town. Not partners anymore, but we meet and we talk.

Dickering for vegetables in the market place.
Watching my children dance.
Walking though the lush grass of my fields.

"It has been a great hardship, Bildad. My holdings are a fraction of what they have been. I have had to work my fingers to the bone."

"It was a devastating loss! The mob was clamouring for blood! I am lucky to have gotten away with my life!"

"Bildad, you are amazing. You are certainly resilient. You seem to have recovered from our disaster much sooner than I."

Have you never trusted anyone?

Why do these people call you their friend?
In which of your relationships have you given the benefit of the doubt?

Zophar and I. When we were young and sharing our dreams.
Springtime in the meadow. Trickling waters, waving grass, a mountain breeze.
Zophar and I stolling from pen to pen as we talk. First to the pen where my lambs are kept; then to the pen where his lambs are kept. All of my ewes and rams seem healthy; all of his flock seem healthy as well. Both flocks graze on the side of the mountain all summer long. The only thing that we don't share in common are the men. I close my eyes and think and think. I am barely able to hear what Zophar is saying. If you wish to end the agreement, Job, that would be fine with me! You need not buy your rams from among my herd! You need not summer your sheep in my meadow anymore! I try to concentrate on the mystery of the defective lambs. Feeble, puny, underweight. Very few will reach adult size. My herd is remaining stable. It is not increasing in size. I cannot keep them and I cannot sell them. The word is abroad among all the dealers not to buy my lambs. I am shunned by every trader in the nearby lands. Zophar is talking as I am thinking, but I hear no words. How is he managing his flock? How is he managing this flock of mine! What kind of magic is he practicing on me? He follows me to my donkey. I angrily wave him away. An agreement is an agreement! I remain a man of my word! I said I would buy from you! I said I would always buy from among your flock!

What do you want from your friends?
What do your friends want from you?
What should be given in a friendship and what withheld?

"I want no more generous offers! I want to know what is going on! Why are your lambs always so healthy and mine so poor!"

"We will pool this year's lambs together. You yourself shall divide the lambs, into the poorest and the best. I will gladly take my half of the poorest ones."

"I do not wish to share your good fortune! I only want what is rightfully mine! I will take my lambs as they come from the hand of God!"

I fumble with the compass! I stagger from cloud to cloud! Acres of bog and water! Leagues of undulating sand! I throw myself on my knees! I smooth a spot in the wind-swept sand! I take the compass in both my hands! I pause and take a deep breath! I wait for my heart to be still! Calm and deliberate is the key! I have been too hasty and careless in my efforts thus far! I reach down and begin my work, but my efforts are all in vain! Each time I seem to have a purchase in the sand, the compass slips from my grasp and slides away! It tumbles over uselessly and all thoughts that I have of creation are stifled and lie stillborn in my brain! I have my eye, my hand and my mind! They have always worked for me, but I fumble here in the void with all of my faculties stripped away, and I cannot make this compass stand up in the sand!

The desert sands are always shifting. Those who know them have come to terms. There is lore that will help one survive on the desert sands.

And God blessed them, and God said vnto them, Be fruitfull, and multiply, and replenish the earth, and subdue it, and haue dominion ouer the fish of the sea, and ouer the foule of the aire, and ouer euery liuing thing that mooueth vpon the earth.

"Who has sent you? What is your name?"
The little boy never answers. He merely nods or shakes his head. Perhaps he doesn't know how to speak our language. He fills our bowl and replenishes our water and he is gone.
He only appears when there is no one else around. Only we five have ever seen the little boy. Does he leave footprints in the ashes and the dust?

It is a curse to have to create a world of one's own! There will be no other people unless I create them! Yet I have absolutely no conception of how to begin! How could anyone stick this compass into a wisp of mist – or sand or rock or bog – and create a human? Why are there no other people with me? I don't like to work alone! Why must all the ideas be mine? I trudge and trudge for miles and miles and I see no one who can help me to create a world! I alone am charged with the task of creating humankind! Why must I be the one to agonize? Why could I not have been created as one among millions of men and women and children? Then I could have asked all of them what they thought! Why have I been chosen to do this? Why choose one who is so inadequate to the task? I would rather find a place where I can lie down and rest, and set these cursed calipers aside!

God causes the cry of the poor to come unto him.
He hears the cry of the afflicted.

We wonder.

The cobbler makes sandals in the marketplace.
He makes them only for those who walk a straight path.
Boys who gather firewood; girls who fetch water at wells.
No one ever asks the cobbler for repairs.

Keren, our third daughter. The child of a difficult birth.
Only days before the accident. A pleasant day. A triumphant moment.
I lurk and watch her from the shadows. She toils at the well. I saw her coming from the house, with her mother's water jug on her shoulder, and ducked back into the shadows to

watch her travail. Keren was not expected to live. My wife had fallen from a donkey. She was in pain for most of her labour. It was feared that mother and child would both lose their lives. Keren struggled into the daylight. She has been struggling ever since. She chooses her struggles carefully, but she is determined that she will lead a normal life. Keren, our third daughter, our youngest child, our greatest worry. Small, white and sickly. She grew slowly and was frequently ill, but with a spirit that demanded to be admired. A drive that overcomes her weaknesses. A determination to live her life as best she can. She is leaning over the well; struggling to raise the bucket; straining at the rope with all her might. I stand here in the shadows and watch her strain. I can feel the pain in her shoulders; I can feel the rope in her palms; I can sense the frown on her brow from this far away. Tempted to move from the shadows. Tempted to help her with her chore. Knowing that she needs to be left alone to struggle with her burden. Knowing that she has come to the well at a time when she feels she will be alone. Struggling to find out something about herself. Finally, she raises the bucket and puts her arms around it and wrestles it onto the rim of the well. She holds the water jug beneath the bucket and struggles to tip the bucket over and spill the gushing water into the jug. Much of it falls on the ground, but much of it lands in the jug. She tips the bucket back with one hand and lets it fall into the well. She grasps the jug with both hands and raises it slowly up to her shoulder. I can feel the tension in her arms; I can feel the sweat on her brow; I can feel the radiant triumph on her face. I turn in the shadows and scurry back to the house.

Stars as bright as can be - gather my thoughts together - god's unsearchable greatness - to create a world of one's own - he spoke and the locusts came - gives life and takes it away - the wearisomeness of life - the cry of the afflicted - he contemplated chaos - an appeal for fair treatment.

"Come, my wife, leave your cooking and come with me! I want you to stand at the door! There is someone I want you to greet!"

"What is it you want of me? I am too busy to play your games! Do you know that someone has taken the water jug?"

"Keren is coming from the well! I want us to meet her as she arrives! I want us both to acknowledge what she has done!"

A young man polishing a knife.
A mother who is aware of her daughter's sighs.
A man enduring the good-will of his friends.

I see no sign of any kind of civilization as I drift helplessly through acres and acres of nothing but air! Not one town or rural establishment! Not one hoofprint or sign of a sandal on a trail! Not one tiny light in the distance to suggest that there is a human alive in this void! Are there no wives? Are there no children? Are there no villages with elders meeting in council? Are there no workers in the fields? Does no one have friends from other towns? A simple goat-boy on a hillside playing a pipe would be nice to see! What I would give to meet a human! Of any nation or any tribe! Perhaps a stream of gurgling water, with a few sticks built up into a tiny pyramid, and a fire bringing a kettle to a boil! And a man hovering patiently, blowing on a tiny flame, as his wife and little children notice me and hustle into the tent and peer from the door! Why is no other human here to welcome me? I would be tempted to trade this compass for a day in the wilderness with those old worn-out beings whom I turned out of my employ, refusing to let them work for crumbs as human sheepdogs! I feel so all alone! There is nothing here but void! Will I never, ever hear another voice?

Surely he shall deliuer thee from the snare of the fouler: and from the noisome pestilence.
Hee shall couer thee with his feathers, and vnder his wings shalt thou trust: his trueth shall bee thy shield and buckler.

We doubt.

Putting on the robe and diadem of judgement.
Providing food to the raven.
Setting the dominion of heaven in the earth.

Young Elihu finishes speaking and clears his throat. He reaches for the water flask.

Everyone attempts to be my comforter. My wife, Eliphaz, Bildad, Zophar. Now, Elihu, the first-born son of my old friend, Barachel. Each one speaks with great fervour to the matter at hand. And after every speech of depth and of wisdom, Job – the wise, the grave, the thoughtful – speaks in return. The boy is just as wise as his elders. What do any of us know of the thoughts of God?

Still, the young man has spoken so passionately. The son of my oldest and dearest friend. A child at whose birth I rejoiced when I heard the news. A child for whom I thanked God for answering Barachel's prayers. He has left his father in jeopardy. He has come here in respect and has spoken the words of his heart. He has spoken in aid of his father's oldest friend. He has spoken what he has come to believe is the truth. Young and fervent, alert and thoughtful, vibrant and keen. He knows as much as any of us knows. Human words are all he has. Human words are all any of us have. It is God that I wish to speak to. To this young man what can I possibly say in return?

An elder brother spoke feebly on his deathbed.
My inheritance to you my younger brother.
And some wisdom that I acquired too late to use.
Never speak in jest when you give your word.

"Many years ago, I was travelling an unfamiliar trail. I met your father and we travelled along together as we made our way towards his home. And as we travelled, we talked. And as we talked, we shared our dreams. I felt that he understood my dreams completely – what I wanted to establish here on earth during my lifetime, and how everything that I did and thought and said went into that enterprise. Your father echoed my thoughts as we moved along, and I felt that I came to know his deepest dreams. As we neared his home, we pledged that we would be friends for the rest of our lives, and that, in time of need, we would heed each other's call. We never met again, but sent greetings from time to time, and indications of the status of our developing dreams – the births of sons and daughters, the building up of herds and lands, our growing status in our communities. I rejoiced when I heard the news of your birth, as your father, no doubt, rejoiced when he heard such news from me. And now, in my hour of need, I send for Barachel and find that he is incapacitated. And as a token of his friendship, he sends you, his first-born son. You have spoken from your heart, which I appreciate. You have given me advice which you would give to your own father or to your own son. You are sincere; you are blunt; you are forthright. I thank you for the fervour with which you speak. If this plague is ever lifted from my head, my first act will be to visit your father – Barachel, my friend for life – in his time of need."

The life of the village - naked shall I return - those who walk a straight path - god's wisdom; man's blindness - a fire was kindled in their company - i seem to be alone - god's righteousness; man's unrighteousness - struggling to find out something - my life is in ashes - my heart is wounded within me.

Time to bring this chaos to order! Time to end this temporary confusion and get my thoughts together and begin to make a world! If only I had someone to talk to about the task that I have been given! About how difficult it is and how I have tried! I have cried out unto the wilderness! I am Job! – do you hear me? – Job! I cry out but no one answers! It is like shouting into a void! Will I never see another person unless I create one? I am determined to keep myself calm! To gather my wits about me! To keep my pulse from fluttering and to keep my heart from beating so wildly! The first step is to conquer myself! Up until now, I have been my own enemy! All of my faculties have been at odds! Let me concentrate and focus! I am determined to create a world! I will circumscribe its boundaries! Then I can contemplate my next step! Surely that would be to lay a cornerstone!

A man with his son on an altar. A man with his son in tears. A man with his knife raised over the heart of his son.

Two figures struggling on a rocky ledge.
Two young men with a fool-proof plan.

A little girl standing beside her older brother.

The voice of an angel. The voice of an angel saying something about his son. What is the voice saying about the son and the knife?

Thou shalt not bee afraid for the terrour by night: nor for the arrow that flieth by day.
Nor for the pestilence that walketh in darknes: nor for the destruction that wasteth at noone-day.

A man with a reprieve. A man with a precious son. A man with a reprieve from his god.

And what to make of this young Elihu, the first-born son of my old friend, Barachel?
An interesting thought occurs. If his father has been a brigand, does young Elihu ply his trade as a brigand too?

What is a cornerstone?
What is it designed to do?
Of what is it made?

We affirm.

Tears of rage and tears of frustration! Why has this impossible task been laid on me? How to create lush fields and fertile valleys? How to create hearths with fires and pots of stew? How to create a world in which other people can live? This ancient compass has proven entirely useless to me! I cannot seem to find a place where I can anchor one arm of the compass in order to allow me to circumscribe the world that I want to create! I have tried so many times and failed to do so! Tears of frustration and tears of futility! Many, many times I have wiped the tears from my eyes and wiped the sweat from my brow and tried again! What is my alternative? Am I condemned to be floating aimlessly through this void for millions of years? Chaos is all around me, stretching forever as far as I know! I have tried and tried and tried! I will the chaos into order – I will it over and over again – but there is never any response to what I do! I cannot make this compass work! I cannot make a mark in the void! Chaos is chaos and it seems it will always be!

Chapter 15

Am I standing on a cloud? A slight breeze is blowing! What is holding me up? I seem to be alone! Where is Eliphaz? Where is Bildad? Is there no one else around? Where are Zophar and Elihu? The breeze begins to quicken! A sound invades my ears! Is it a thunder-clap or a voice? What is it saying? My ears begin to ache! The breeze increases steadily and soon becomes a blast! The wind tears at my face! The voice gets louder and louder! My ears feel ready to explode! The voice is booming in my ears! I cannot make out any words! Where is the ash-heap? Where are the others? Am I alone?

I will articulate my cause! I know that I will be justified!

A woman who raises ten children with her husband.
A man who is waiting for word from the land of the Buzites.
Five men sharing a bowl with scraps of food.

Withdraw thine hand from me! Let not thy dread make me afraid!

Facing the thing which I greatly fear.
Listening to the timbrel and the harp.
Making a request of my God.

Call and I will answer! Let me speak and answer thou me!

What do you want to say to God?
What does God want to say to you?
What are the ways in which one can speak without saying a word?

I don't know where I am standing! I don't know what is beneath my feet! Rock? Sand? Wisps of cloud? It feels like I am sinking down in quick-sand! It feels like I am dangling in the air! It feels like I am whirling over and over – head over head over heels –

and yet I get the feeling that I am standing still! A voice assaults my ears and a wind rips at my skin! It tears at my hair and at my clothing! I can feel the blood come pouring out of my ears! I cry out in my agony! The fierce wind drowns my cry! The fierce tempest ravishes my ears!

God preserveth not the life of the wicked.
He giveth right to the poor.

We flourish.

A leader of a caravan studies some bleaching bones.
Rib bones, leg bones, skull.
The bones of a large bird in the desert sand.

Sitting on the ash-heap. The five of us.
Village life goes on. The city gates, the market square, the rows of vendors. The noise and the actions of a busy day.
A spurt of dust in front of the ash-heap. A tiny whirlwind gathering speed. The five of us look at one another. Do you see what I am seeing? The dust whirls faster and faster. We look on in amazement. It is dancing back and forth in front of us. No one near us seems to notice. Perhaps it is only we who are able to see. The whirlwind circles in fury without a sound. I stare and stare and stare. Finally, a voice speaks out of the whirlwind. Clear and calm and firm.

An armload of firewood - threescore years and ten - the sense, however, is clear - a tiny whirlwind gathering speed - the pains of hell gat hold upon me - a thousand years in thy sight - such omissions furnish important evidence - wisdom in the inward parts - this is the day which the lord hath made - my skin is on fire.

"Who is this that darkneth counsel by words without knowledge? Gird up now thy loins like a man, for I will demand of thee, and answer thou me. Where wast thou when I laid the foundations of the earth? Declare, if thou hast understanding. Who hath laid the measures thereof, if thou knowest? Or who hath stretched the line upon it? Whereupon are the foundations thereof fastened? Or who laid the cornerstone thereof, when the morning stars sang together and all the sons of God shouted for joy? Hast thou commanded the morning and caused the day to know his place? Hast thou entered the springs of the sea? Hast thou perceived the breadth of the earth? Hath the rain a father? Who hath begotten the drops of dew? Out of whose womb came the ice? Knowest thou the ordinances of heaven? Canst thou set the dominion thereof in the earth? Who hath put wisdom in the inward parts? Who hath given understanding to the heart? Knowest thou because thou wast then born? Or because the number of thy days is great? Doth the hawk fly by thy wisdom and stretch her wings towards the south? Doth the eagle mount up at thy command and make her nest on high? Shall he that contendeth with the Almighty instruct him? He that reproveth God let him answer. Speak if thou hast understanding. If thou art equal to me in knowledge, answer thou me."

Make a ioyfull noise vnto the Lord, all ye lands.
Serue the Lord with gladnes: come before his presence with singing.

My eyes are stricken blind! There is nothing I can see! I don't know where I am standing! I hear a fantastic roaring in my ears! My hair and clothes are being clawed at by the wind! My skin feels like it is melting! I can feel my blood trickling down through the cage of my bones! My ears are as big as my head! The voice is booming louder! A relentless, insistent drumming! Every word is a thunder-clap! Every syllable rattles my brain! Is there no one to share my agony? This is more than I can bear! I wish that I could faint dead away! I wish that I could die and be at peace!

Thou shalt know that thy seed shall be great.
And thine offspring as the grass of the earth.

We falter.

God looked every creature in the eye.
Every human and every living thing.
I contribute more than you to life on the earth.
Look around you and you will see my list.

The whirlwind spins like a child's top but it offers no more words.

Cattle, donkeys, camels. Laughter, haggling, chatter. The life of the village goes on across the square.

My throat is dry as dust. I gather my scattered thoughts – I am determined that I will speak – but a voice beside me shoulders my thoughts aside.

Being feet for the lame.
Breaking the jaws of the wicked.
Giving the horse his strength.

"We beg leave to speak, oh Lord. We are the three friends of thy servant, Job: Eliphaz the Temanite, Bildad the Shuhite and Zophar the Naamathite. We acknowledge that thy wrath is kindled against us. We acknowledge that we have not spoken of thee the thing that is right to say, as thy servant, Job, hath done in thy hearing. We bow down to thee, Oh Lord, and make unto thee a solemn pledge to take unto us now seven bullocks and seven rams, and to go to thy servant Job and to offer up for ourselves a burnt offering, and to plead with thy servant Job to pray for us, for we have come to believe that thou hast accepted him, lest thou deal with us after our folly, in that we have come to believe that we have not spoken of thee the thing which is right – again my Lord, unlike thy servant, Job. We bow down to thee in obeisance. These things we humbly ask in thy name, oh Lord."

Do these people speak for you?
Are their thoughts the same as yours?
What are the words that you are struggling so hard to say?

Pinned flat against the sun! My legs are dangling down! A fierce wind presses against my chest! My back is burning as if I am lying on hot coals! Is anybody with me? My sweat drips down onto my chest! My skin bubbles and blisters as if on fire! Beside me, I catch a glimpse of a hand and a wrist! I turn my head again! Another hand and wrist! Who is it who is with me? I reach out, but I am not able to touch! The fierce wind fans the flames! Surely my hair is on fire! The raucous cacophony thunders against my ears!

A wadi is never the same. It gives life and takes it away. There is no one who is an expert on wadi lore.

And God saw euery thing that hee had made: and behold, it was very good.

How I long to fall asleep. If only I could dream. I long to fall asleep and dream of the little boy.

Who is this person who appears before me? Is it someone I used to know? The person does not speak! The person has lips but they are not open! The voice is coming from somewhere else! Is it Eliphaz? Is is Bildad? Is it Zophar? Is it Elihu, Barachel's boy? The person blazes in shining radiance! No one I know could look like this! Is it one of the ancient prophets? Is it an angel come from heaven? How do they look? How do they dress? Is it my wife? Is it one of our children, come back from the dead? The voice is loud! The voice is insistent! The voice is booming! The voice is demanding but I cannot make out the words! If only this person would speak! I would know what the voice intends! Why am I forced to listen? Why are the voice and the person not clear to my ears and my eyes?

Lift up thy face unto God.
Make thy prayer unto him and he shall hear thee.

We gain.

A mule and a human rode along.
I have had another thought said the mule.
If God were to hear and start to make changes,
What other changes might he make to the universe?

The whirling dust-cloud spins like a top.
It draws no eyes; it makes no sound. No one in the village shows concern.
I try to swallow, but I have no spittle. Before I can speak, the silence is broken again.

The sound of the trumpet - psalms of elation and sadness - taking things as they come or go - make a joyfull noise - filling their water flasks - give me understanding - no more words - practical skill in the direction of life and its affairs - the number of his years - thou art good and doest good.

"We beg leave to speak again, oh Lord. We are the three friends of thy servant, Job: Eliphaz the Temanite, Bildad the Shuhite and Zophar the Naamathite. We humbly beseech thee, oh Lord, that thou shalt turn the captivity of Job, when Job has prayed for his friends. That thou shalt give unto Job twice as much as he had before. That there shalt come unto him all his brethren, and all his sisters, and all they that have been of his acquaintance before, and eat bread with him in his house. And that they shalt bemoan him and comfort him over all the evil that thee, the Lord, hast brought upon him. That every man shalt also give him a piece of money, and every one an ear-ring of gold. We pray also, oh Lord, that thou shalt bless the latter end of Job more than his beginning, with fourteen thousand sheep, six thousand camels, a thousand yoke of oxen and a thousand she-asses. Restore to him his family. Let him have seven sons and three daughters, as he had before. And let him call the name of the first, Jemima, and the name of the second, Kezia, and the name of the third, Keren-happuch. And let there be in all the land no women found so fair as the daughters of Job. And let their father give them inheritance among their brethren. Let thy servant Job live an hundred and forty years, and see his sons and his sons's sons, even unto four generations. Let Job die, oh Lord, being old and full of days. All this we beseech thee, Lord, in thy holy name."

A young man who waits for time to ripen.
A young shepherd with a perfect method for raising sheep.
Ten children telling stories as they eat and drink.

The wind is a ferocious blast! Bits and pieces of debris fly past my face! A tiny flower smacks my chest! My heart stops beating for a moment! I try to raise my hand! The pressure of the wind against my limbs is ferocious! My hand moves slowly, as if in molasses! I strain to raise it to my chest! I have almost reached the flower – bright yellow with fluttering petals – when the wind shifts ever so slightly and the flower leaves my chest and is lost in the gale!

I feel the tears form in my eyes! The torrent flattens them against my cheeks! A loud voice pounds and pounds against my ears!

Know ye that the Lord, hee is God, it is he that hath made vs, and not we our selues: wee are his people, and the sheepe of his pasture.
Enter into his gates with thanksgiuing, and into his Courts with praise: bee thankfull vnto him, and blesse his Name.

We lose.

Thinking of the flower which is cut down.
Putting another log on the fire.
Crying aloud for judgement.

The whirlwind spins in the dust in front of the ash-heap.

Not a sound from the village. Not a sound from the whirlwind. Not a sound from the four who sit with me.

My throat is raw. I try to swallow, but I have no spittle to whet my voice. I open my lips. They are cracked and dry as I lick them with my tongue. The whirlwind spins like a child's top in the dust. I gather my thoughts together and then I speak.

A small voice spoke up from the back of the room.
It was a very tiny cloud who was extremely shy.
There are so many humans; there is only so much rain.
Which humans should we favour? Which deny?

"What shall I answer thee? I lay my hand upon my mouth. I proceed no further. I know, Lord, that thou canst do everything, and that no thought can be withholden from thee. I have uttered that which I have understood not. Things too wonderful for me, which I knew not. I have heard of thee by the hearing of the ear, but now mine eye seeth thee. Wherefore I abhor myself and repent in dust and ashes."

A young man buying sheep - my hour of need - I have hoped in thy word - what is there to be done but to speculate - looked every creature in the eye - my soul is continually in my hand - everything that hath breath - the problem is simpler if we omit the dubius sections - bright yellow with fluttering petals - the number of his years.

I am standing in the field where my oxen are plowing and my asses are feeding! The Sabeans are falling upon them and taking them away! My wife and our children and our children's children are standing with me! Noach's littlest one is clinging to my hand! The wind tears at our clothing and a roaring assaults our ears! We are standing in the field where the fire of God is falling from heaven and burning up the sheep! We are standing in the field where I keep my camels! The Chaldeans are making three bands and carrying them away! We are standing in a house! Mattan's house! Our sons and our daughters are eating and drinking wine! The great wind comes from the wilderness and brings it down! The pungent smell of burnt wood and smouldering ash! My wife and our children and our children's children are standing with me! The wind is howling and raging and screaming in our ears! We are standing in the field where I love to dream! The field with green grass and grazing ewes and a trickling rivulet! We gather our children to us! They bury their heads in our shoulders and clutch at our robes! The wind is a howling, raging torrent! A tempest of great ferocity! Our family huddles closely together! We fuse together tightly and face the wind!

An old man whose hands are shaking. An old man who lives in torment. An old man who trembles at what he has done.

The sheep-market in the land of the Naamathites.
A man who strains to read the message in another's eyes.
Children being shooed like a gaggle of geese.

Two sons. A ritual blessing. A shattered dream.

For the Lord is good, his mercy is euerlasting: and his trueth endureth to all generations.

An old man who is broken and blind. An old man who shakes his head. An old man who cannot believe what has come to pass.

What is the meaning of the whirlwind?
What is the purpose of the still, small voice?
Who are you to claim that you hear the voice of God?

We endure.

The wind dies down and I am lying, prostrate, on the ground! The wind becomes a breeze and I struggle up and try to get my balance! The booming voice grows faint and fades away! I press my feet into firm earth and look around me! Eliphaz! Bildad! Zophar! Elihu too! All are sitting on the ash-heap and looking around! There is a ringing in my ears! We are all of us blinking our eyes! Around us we see the village! People moving to and fro! Donkeys, camels, hawkers, beggars! A lady haggling with a melon-seller! A dog scratching fleas! The voice is gone!

Chapter 16

The departure of my friends. Eliphaz, Bildad, Zophar and Elihu.
Five people sitting on an ash-heap.

Tightening up their saddles. Filling their water flasks. Eliphaz to the land of the Temanites. Bildad to the land of the Shuites. Zophar to the land of the Naahamites. Elihu, son of Barachel, to the land of the Buzites. A long trek for each over difficult terrain.

My skin is on fire. My life is in ashes. My children are dead.

Naked came I out of my mother's womb.

The earth was without form and void.
Darkness was upon the face of the deep.
The spirit of the Lord hovered over the waters.

Naked shall I return.

Tending to the needs of my flocks and my herds.
Overseeing the preparations of my travelling caravans.
Enjoying my three daughters and my seven sons.

The Lord giveth and the Lord taketh away. Blessed is the name of the Lord.

What was God's plan when he decided to create the universe?
What was he thinking when he contemplated chaos?
What were his hopes as he took the calipers in hand?

The departure of Eliphaz, Bildad, Zophar and Elihu.
Five people sitting and talking on an ash-heap.

Each has come from his own place. Each has come to mourn with me. Leaving business behind, leaving acquaintances behind, leaving family behind.

Each of them has come to me in my hour of need. They assumed that I would do the same for them.

God is greater than man.

We hope.
We laugh.
We flourish.

Double to win. Double to win.
This is my motto. Double to win.
The choice is between the skull or the skin.
This is my motto. Double to win.

Not much more than a babe in arms.

My father and my mother and all my relatives sitting around a big fire. A black sky above and stars as bright as can be.

A hand reaches out from time to time and stirs the fire with a stick. Flames jet out and the fire breathes and spreads to other logs. A young boy gets up from time to time and gathers an armload of firewood from the pile on the edge of the darkness and tosses them carefully and strategically onto the fire. The flames flicker on the faces. I am in my mother's arms, listening to the chanting. Men, women, children, chanting the words of the ancient prayers. The sparks rise up and drift and fade away. Our words rise up to the heavens. An elder chants and everyone chants in reply.

Eating and drinking wine - a cry from inside the house - thou hast shewed thy people hard things - naked came i - the misfortune of the pious - incline thine eare unto me - why standeth thou afar off, o lord - interview with god - oxen plowing and asses feeding - absolutely unprovoked by sin.

"Praise ye the Lord. Praise God in his sanctuary. Praise him in the firmament of his power."

"Praise him for his mighty acts. Praise him according to his excellent greatness."

"Praise him with the sound of the trumpet. Praise him with the psaltery and harp."

"Praise him with the timbrel and dance. Praise him with stringed instruments and organs."

"Praise him upon the loud cymbals. Praise him upon the high sounding cymbals."

"Let every thing that hath breath praise the Lord."

My God, my God, why hast thou forsaken mee? Why art thou so far from helping me, and from the words of my roaring?

O my God, I crie in the day time, but thou hearest not; and in the night season, and am not silent.

The departure of my friends. Each preparing for a long and difficult journey.
Two men meeting a young girl at a well.
Eliphaz removing the feed-bag from his donkey.

"The weather looks fine for travel."
"I came as soon as I heard."
"May God be your guide as you make your way."

Behold God is great and we know him not.
Neither can the number of his years be searched out.

We fear.
We cry.
We falter.

A tree grew in the forest.
It reached its leaves towards the sky.
But it never got there.

I am a young boy, in the darkness, sitting at my father's side. Old enough to gather firewood. Old enough to tend the family fire.

My mother beside my father. Around the fire, my brothers and my sisters. Our family circle in the darkness of the night.

Once in a while, I get up and get an armload of firewood and place each piece precisely and strategically on the fire. We are in a field near the mountains. A lush valley in the springtime. Or perhaps a stubble field at harvest time. Above us there are stars. Around us there is darkness. I lean over and blow against the embers and the wood glows red in the darkness and the sparks leap up and sail past my shoulder and above my head. My father and my mother chant psalms of elation and sadness, hope and fear, delivery and despair, as we children respond with each verse. As I chant along with my family, I watch the sparks drift upwards and fade into the darkness of the night. We chant the psalms of our ancestors and ourselves.

Forming myself out of clay.

Granting audience to those who would speak with me.
Giving an account of all my matters.

"Lord, thou hast been our dwelling place in all generations."

"Before the mountains were brought forth, or ever thou hadst formed the earth and the world, even from everlasting to everlasting, thou art God."

"Thou turnest man to destruction; and sayest, Return, ye children of men."

"For a thousand years in thy sight are but as yesterday when it is past, and as a watch in the night."

"Thou carriest them away as with a flood; they are as a sleep: in the morning they are like grass which groweth up."

"In the morning it flourisheth, and groweth up; in the evening it is cut down, and withereth."

"For we are consumed by thine anger, and by thy wrath are we troubled."

"Thou hast set our iniquities before thee, our secret sins in the light of thy countenance."

"For all our days are passed away in thy wrath: we spend our years as a tale that is told."

"The days of our years are threescore years and ten; and if by reason of strength they be fourscore years, yet is their strength labour and sorrow; for it is soon cut off, and we fly away."

"Who knoweth the power of thine anger? Even according to thy fear, so is thy wrath."

"So teach us to number our days, that we may apply our hearts unto wisdom."

Did God create the world for you?
Did God create the world for others?
Did God create the world for himself?

The departure of my friends.
Two young men sipping cold water and hatching a plan.
Bildad checking the water in his gourds.

"Better to talk than to suffer in silence."
"I appreciate all that was said."
"No one should have to suffer alone at a time like this."

The mountains are always there. They were there long before us. They will be there long after we pass away.

The desert sands are always shifting. They are like the waves of the sea. Waves of sand engulf and waves of sand recede.

A wadi is never the same. It is life when rain is plenty. It is death when the rains are withheld.

In the beginning God created the Heauen, and the Earth.

A crowd of children is gathered at the gate to watch them go. A dozen or so, perhaps.
Is the little boy among them? Too far away for me to distinguish. My eyes are not of the best. Do I dare to walk towards them? What is it that I need to see?
Perhaps he is there; perhaps he is not. He has been here; I know; I saw him every day. Not a word; no explanation. A draught of cool water and a few meager scraps in a wooden bowl.

The departure of my friends.
A young man buying sheep from his new friend.
Zophar checking the hoof on his mule.

"I was shocked when I heard the news."
"You were kind to come to my side."
"Being together is a blessing in itself."

Thou shalt have thy delight in the Almighty.
Thou shalt lift up thy face unto God.

We rejoice.
We wonder.
We gain.

You say that you want to talk, my brother.
Though silence was golden before.
It is words that leave the deepest wounds.
I would rather you use a knife.

Myself, my wife and all of our children. Ten children sent from God. A gift of plenty.
We sit in a circle around the fire. The night is dark. Perhaps a moon. There are many stars.
Our eldest son has the tending of the fire. From time to time, he takes a stick and pokes at the embers and turns a log over to expose the burnt side to the air and it sparks into fire and spreads to other logs. Our youngest son is in charge of gathering the firewood. Our youngest daughter always helps him as best she may. The world is full; the world is plentiful; the world is good. Ten children, a faithful wife, an abundance of herds and flocks and fields.

The sun comes up each morning and the rains come in season and the crops yield their bounty at harvest time. Twelve of us in the glow of a crackling fire. Above us the darkness and the stars. God in his heaven and we as his family, here on the ground. My wife and I take turns chanting the psalms. Our children chant lustily in reply.

Blackened and burning carcases - witnesses of the creation - preserve me, o god - the morning sun - women and children weeping - if mules were human - the most to be dreaded of sins - as carefree as they seem - I have set the lord always before me - when i am old and gray headed - sheep and servants consumed by fire.

"O Lord, our Lord, how excellent is thy name in all the earth! who hast set thy glory above the heavens."

"When I consider thy heavens, the work of thy fingers, the moon and the stars, which thou hast ordained;"

"What is man, that thou art mindful of him? and the son of man, that thou visitest him?"

"For thou hast made him a little lower than the angels, and hast crowned him with glory and honour."

"Thou madest him to have dominion over the works of thy hands; thou hast put all things under his feet:"

"All sheep and oxen, yea, and the beasts of the field."

"The fowl of the air, and the fish of the sea, and whatsoever passeth through the paths of the seas."

"O Lord, our Lord, how excellent is thy name in all the earth!"

Ancient calipers of brass and of wood.
God created the heavens and the earth.
The Lord God formed man of the dust of the earth.

The departure of my friends.
A traveller trapped on a ledge with a broken leg.
Elihu checking the cinch on his horse.

"I just had to break my silence."
"You said what you had to say."
"My father insisted that I come and be with you."

All they that see me, laugh me to scorne: they shoote out the lippe, they shake the head, saying,

He trusted on the Lord, that he would deliuer him. Let him deliuer him, seeing he delighted in him.

We mourn.
We doubt.
We lose.

Chatting cheerfully in the marketplace.
Offering advice in the gatherings of the elders.
Worshipping my God.

Myself and my wife. Just the two of us, now that our children are gone.

I make a fire at night. Near our tent in the fields. Or in the fire-pit near our dwelling in the town.

We sit beside the fire. The night is dark and the stars shine bright as jewels. I take a stick and stir the embers and little flames leap up and sparks break away and drift above our heads. Just the two of us alone. No ancestral gathering, nor childhood clan, nor our own family gathered around the fire. We think our thoughts and seldom speak. The loss of our children is great, but not to be dwelt on. We each know what the other is thinking. What need to be constantly saying what we constantly think? Enough that we sit and think our thoughts by the fire. At the end of the evening, we chant the words of a psalm. I chant and my wife chants in return.

A young shepherd had a wise friend.
The wise friend gave the young shepherd advice.
If ever you are menaced by a fierce wolf, reach out and stroke him under the chin.
He will become placid. Almost a friend.

"The Lord is my shepherd; I shall not want."

"He maketh me to lie down in green pastures: he leadeth me beside the still waters."

"He restoreth my soul: he leadeth me in the paths of righteousness for his name's sake."

"Yea, though I walk through the valley of the shadow of death, I will fear no evil: for thou art with me; thy rod and thy staff they comfort me."

"Thou preparest a table before me in the presence of mine enemies: thou anointest my head with oil; my cup runneth over."

"Surely goodness and mercy shall follow me all the days of my life: and I will dwell in the house of the Lord for ever."

A great wind from the wilderness - curse god and die - all scrupulosity of life - our thirsts are quenched - as for god, his way is perfect - a temporary chastisement - god made the flowers - save me from the lion's mouth - a man with a blessing to give - seven sons and three daughters.

The departure of my friends.
A woman who shares ten children with her husband.
My wife and I side-by-side. Standing shoulder-to-shoulder. She has mourned in her own fashion. No doubt she has been lonely while I have grieved. Who supports the female as the female supports the male?

"You came to see me every day."
"You needed water; you needed food."
"You were good to do so."

A man stands on a mountain top and looks out over a plain. His eyes are filled with wonder. A man of hopes, a man of vision, a man of dreams.

Seven sons and three daughters.
Eating and drinking and telling stories in their brother's house.
A great wind came up out of the wilderness.

A man with a son. A man with a precious son. Under the heavy burden of an edict from his god.

I am powred out like water, and all my bones are out of ioynt: my heart is like waxe, it is melted in the middest of my bowels.
My strength is dried vp like a potsheard: and my tongue cleaueth to my iawes; and thou hast brought me into the dust of death.

An old man who is now blind. An old man at the end of his life. An old man with trembling hands and failing eyes.

There has been no news of Barachel since Elihu arrived. No word from the land of the Buzites. Perhaps Barachel will be there, when Elihu returns, to welcome him at the gate. Or perhaps sad faces will announce my friend's demise.

God speed Elihu homeward. I pray for the reunion of a healthy father and his loving son.

Do you believe in God?

Do you believe that God made humankind?
Do you believe that God made the universe and all that is in it?

We pray.
We affirm.
We endure.

The departure of my friends.
A man shaking dust and ash from a ragged robe.

I wave as they ride through the gate. Eliphaz, Bildad, Zophar and Elihu. Each takes a different direction towards his home. I stand beside my wife and watch them go. Shepherds herd their sheep into pens; handlers make up caravans; vendors hawk their wares in the marketplace. Children play in the dust and the dung. The life of the village continues on.

Three Books

Job: The Cornerstone of the Universe – a novel

Wracked by fever, tormented by boils, devastated by the loss of his entire family, the wretched Job cries out to the heavens. Why has his God forsaken him? Why do such things happen here on earth? Why is the universe so flawed? Why are human beings subjected to such agonizing torments? He shakes his fist at the sky and demands a personal audience. His agony has given him the questions. He insists on hearing the answers from the mouth of God.

The Making of the Cornerstone of the Universe – a reflective journal

This journal records my reflections on the process of the crafting of the novel as it evolved through the stages of planning, writing, editing and polishing. It constitutes an effort to be as conscious as possible of the process whereby the single idea that suggested the topic of the novel was expanded into a complex work of art. Topics range from the nuts and bolts of novel-building to the nature of the novel as an art-form.

Planning the Cornerstone of the Universe – a planning notebook

During the writing of the novel, I kept a hand-written notebook which records the day-by-day development of the novel as it found its shape and style. The notebook – now in print form – reveals how a vast cluster of thoughts was sifted, selected, structured and polished into novel-form.

The Project

Together, this novel, journal and notebook comprise the seventeenth installment in an on-going novel-writing project in which I am exploring the concept of form and meaning in the novel, and of the novel as a form of expression in the 21st Century. All of the published journals and notebooks are available for free download at www.johnpass-field.ca.

About the Author

John Passfield was born in St. Thomas, Ontario, Canada, and continues to reside in Southern Ontario, near Cayuga, with his family. He has taught and studied literature, creative writing and drama, and is interested in the development of the novel as an art-form.

Novels by John Passfield

Grave Song
The Agony of Robert Chisholm

Jumbo
P. T. Barnum's Greatest Creation

Pinafore Park
The Swan Boat Incident

Water Lane
The Pilgrimage of Christopher Marlowe

Rain of Fire
The Ordeal of Conductor Spettigue

Victoria Day
The Fabric of the Community

The Wright Brothers
Flight is Possible

Leni Riefenstahl
The Valley of the Shadow

Out of the Park
The Cogitations of Babe Ruth

Raskolnikov
Murder with an Axe

Death Day
The Apology of Sergei Eisenstein

Albert Einstein
Wondrous Strange

Geoffrey Chaucer
Canterbury Bound

Ospringe
A Visit with Grandad

Pompeii
Vesuvius Dominus

Beethoven
The Ninth Immersion

Job
The Cornerstone of the Universe

Bethune
The Only Person Alive in the World

Terry Fox
Somewhere the Hurting Must Stop

See www.johnpassfield.ca for publishing information.

In Search of Form and Meaning:
Journals by John Passfield

Each journal is a day-by-day record of the complex process that a writer undergoes while crafting a work of art. It records the largest decisions, of structure and theme, and the smallest decisions, such as the choice of one word over another, and the constant interaction between the two. Each journal is a record of a writer's reflection on the craft of novel-writing.

The Making of Grave Song

The Making of Jumbo

The Making of Pinafore Park

The Making of Water Lane

The Making of Rain of Fire

The Making of Victoria Day

The Making of Flight is Possible

The Making of The Valley of the Shadow

The Making of Out of the Park

The Making of Murder with an Axe

The Making of Death Day

The Making of Wondrous Strange

The Making of Canterbury Bound

The Making of Ospringe

The Making of Vesuvius Dominus

The Making of The Ninth Immersion

The Making of The Cornerstone of the Universe

The Making of The Only Person Alive in the World

The Making of Somewhere the Hurting Must Stop

See www.johnpassfield.ca for publishing information.

The Novel as an Art-Form:
Planning Notebooks by John Passfield

Each planning notebook is a printed version of the hand-written notebook which records the planning, writing, editing and polishing of each novel. Each notebook is an attempt to record, understand, and organize the vast cluster of thoughts which occur as one grapples with the various levels of organization which a clear yet complex work of art demands.

Planning Grave Song

Planning Jumbo

Planning Pinafore Park

Planning Water Lane

Planning Rain of Fire

Planning Victoria Day

Planning Flight is Possible

Planning The Valley of the Shadow

Planning Out of the Park

Planning Murder with an Axe

Planning Death Day

Planning Wondrous Strange

Planning Canterbury Bound

Planning Ospringe

Planning Vesuvius Dominus

Planning The Ninth Immersion

Planning The Cornerstone of the Universe

Planning The Only Person Alive in the World

Planning Somewhere the Hurting Must Stop

See www.johnpassfield.ca for publishing information.

www.ingramcontent.com/pod-product-compliance
Lightning Source LLC
Chambersburg PA
CBHW051839020726
47502CB00005B/1856